One Wreath with Love

By Jan Roffman

One Wreath with Love

JAN ROFFMAN

PUBLISHED FOR THE CRIME CLUB BY
DOUBLEDAY AND COMPANY, INC.
GARDEN CITY, NEW YORK
1978

All of the characters in this book
are fictitious, and any resemblance
to actual persons, living or dead,
is purely coincidental.

ISBN: 0-385-14103-3
Library of Congress Catalog Card Number 77-92230
Copyright © 1978 by Doubleday & Company, Inc.
All Rights Reserved
Printed in the United States of America
First Edition

One Wreath with Love

ONE

Numbed with shock, Edmund had a sense of tumbling, like a
fallen angel being sucked into a vortex. Miraculously the process reversed itself; sheer will-power erected a solid platform beneath his feet. As if mounted on a pinnacle of time he surveyed
not only the present and the past, but the future laid out in a
vast panorama. On a phantom pair of scales he balanced the al-
ternatives: to be ploughed back into the dust of mediocrity or,
against all odds, become a survivor.

Garth Rampton paced the floor, appalled that his trust had
been betrayed by a senior member of his staff guilty of professional malpractice; rocked by the failure in himself to detect a
fatal flaw in an employee who'd not only swindled him, but
smirched an honoured name.

Edmund Lang, with deep inner reserves and a nestful of secrets to hide, was a solitary man. Forty years old, near enough
to six feet, lithe, quick-moving with no surplus fat to encumber
his bones, his movements were neat, exact as though timed in
his head. His features were aquiline with pale skin-tones, and
his mouth, even when he smiled, lacked humour. His light
eyes, not quite blue, not quite grey, were sealed against in-
trusion.

Garth Rampton addressed him in the harsh tone of a school-
master expelling a delinquent pupil. "You will vacate this office
by noon tomorrow. Your salary will be paid until the last day
of the month. You understand?"

Edmund's half-bowed head nodded assent. Even if he'd
wished to speak his voice would have disobeyed his will. At the
heart of his widening vision he had spied the perfect imple-

ment of execution: a marble urn poised on a corner of the drinks cupboard—one of the casual footnotes added by the interior decorator who, on Garth's instructions had transformed a drab, conventional office suite into a seductive scenario for the sale of dreams.

To Edmund it was a back-drop to a drama that, when the curtain fell, would spell either salvation or a living death. The equation was simplicity itself: to kill or be killed.

Moving slantways, the sound of his footsteps was sucked into the inch-deep carpet. To Garth he had become a loathsome creature beyond redemption whom he could not bear to touch, even with a glance. Edmund tensed himself for a second round of denunciation. It was not forthcoming. Instead Garth leaned forward to reach for his lighter that was lying on the far side of the low table: literally offering himself for slaughter. No sound passed his lips as the smooth belly of the urn cracked his skull.

Edmund placed the urn on the table, examined his handiwork. A trickle of blood wound through the grey-black hair, circled the sharp jawbone. He fetched a linen towel from the visitors' wash-room, tied it firmly round the head, tucked in the ends under the chin. A blood-stain the size of a pin's head would have spelt ruin. A burst of exultation that he had, within a minute span of time, wreaked vengeance on his enemy, induced a faint dizziness. He lay prone on the green leather sofa, deliberately schooling himself back to calm. After the short respite, he tipped his body sideways to keep watch on the near-corpse. The breathing was barely perceptible, but it breathed, was live flesh and bone—pliant. Though the room was at the rear of the building, its windows close-netted for privacy, he could hear the honk and squeal of the home-going traffic. 7:15. Bright as day. Before him stretched an enforced wait of five hours.

He allowed himself the relaxation of marvelling on the script that must have lain dormant for years in the depths of his subconscious, yet was instantly to hand in a crisis. He counted it not as luck but as evidence of some unique quality within himself, a super-preparedness; the most potent weapon in any battle. Even the elements favoured him. The previous night, without fore-knowledge of its significance, he'd gazed at the full moon that would give a repeat performance tonight. Fate working for him, against his three-quarters dead enemy.

In his mind he juggled the two cars backwards and forwards until he had slotted them into their appointed rôles. He estimated the distance he'd have to cover on foot as five miles: three miles out and two miles home. A reasonable distance for a man in excellent physical shape, due to his habit of making long solitary treks over the countryside.

A sound from the chair jerked him upright: Garth's hands had slid from the arms onto the seat. He felt the pulse that thrummed irregularly under the pressure of his thumb. He replaced the hands, lifted the bound head. The eyes rolled. He checked that the blood had not seeped through the towel, rewound it tighter. Before the daylight faded he carried the urn into the wash-room, scrubbed it with a nail brush then, enclosing it in a handkerchief, replaced it on top of the drinks cabinet. Garth's fingerprints presented no hazard, demanded no alibi; silently he rehearsed the dialogue that had supposedly passed between them. They had sat facing across the low table, drinks in hand, discussing a property that had recently come on the market. Fingerprints on the table, the leather surface of the chair, on the glasses were admissible. He took two tumblers from the drinks cupboard, pressed Garth's fingers on one, poured a teaspoonful of whisky in each glass and rolled them between his hand to coat them with spirit.

He measured and estimated the weight of the near-corpse. Slightly shorter than average, with the minimum of flesh. Say, ten to eleven stone. With his own superior height, bone and muscle, the task ahead should not be beyond him.

His mouth puckered with contempt. Garth Rampton, a man who prided himself on his honour, business rectitude! An only child, at twenty-five he'd inherited a prosperous firm of estate agents, with three outlets in the area, plus the fortune his miser-father had salted away. Not for him the misery of thwarted ambition, in-fighting with colleagues who threatened to eclipse him. But a petty princeling whose word was law. Now he was dying, dying nicely, silently.

He returned to the sofa, lay there in a state of semi-catalepsy in which his body relaxed but his brain raced in top gear, plugging any minute hole that might arouse the faintest tick of suspicion. Every hour he checked the pulse. Gradually the irregularity became more pronounced. Panic swooped. He felt his teeth clench until his jaws ached. It was vital it sustained a breath of life. Presented with a choice between failure and death, he would have opted for death, oblivion. But the death-script his brain had conceived was written not for him but for Garth Rampton. Slowly his muscles relaxed as he smiled down upon the man who would soon, but not too soon, be dead.

At 12:10 by his luminous watch, he rose from the sofa, stood over Garth, listening, feeling with his fingers the clammy flesh. Fear leapt a second time presenting him with a series of obscene film clips: suppose the half-corpse, against all odds, became mobile, pounded on the window, or plunged through it, recovered sufficiently to crawl on hands and knees for help! He tested the legs: stumps. The head, in the hazy moonlight, lolled like a rag doll's. The pulse maintained its faint uneven beat. He forced himself to breathe evenly, in and out, deliberately slowing his heart-beats. On the last breath he accepted there was a minute element of risk. A gamble, but one in which he held all the cards.

He locked the door of the office, unlocked the connecting door into the car-park, opened its solid wooden gate, by-passed Garth's car, climbed into his own, eased it out, then closed and locked the gate behind him. Avoiding the High Street he turned left, circling the quiet residential roads, the inhabitants of which were not likely to be awake, much less abroad. The High Street by-passed, he joined the road that would lead him home, increased his speed.

*

Faint as it was, the piteous mewling jerked Violet Madden awake, sent her lurching from her chair, left leg crippled by pins and needles, right knee-joint pierced by red-hot stabs of rheumatism. Snatching up a torch, she hobbled to the window, tugged to release the catch, but it was jammed, forcing her to struggle to the front door, calling even before it was open: "Sammy, Sammy, here Sammy love." She plunged into a moon-glazed landscape, crying his name as she limped down the few feet of path to the gate. She was on the other side of it when the blight of memory was rekindled, and Sammy's name died on her tongue. Her sleep-fuddled ears had played a trick on her. There was no Sammy, only a mouldering heap of fragile bones, rotting fur, wrapped in a new cardigan she had never worn, packed in a shoe box Mr. Pritchard had buried under the plum tree. "There, don't you take on so. 'Tisn't good for you, not with you being bereaved. Kittens are ten a penny. Folks are thankful to be rid of them. Give you one for the asking."

"No good will come of it, you mark my words," Dorothea had warned darkly. "You wait till it starts making messes all over the place for you to clean up, because don't imagine I'm going to mop up after an alley-cat. And he'll need doctoring or he'll stink the place out."

Sammy had never made a single mess, and he hadn't lived long enough to be doctored. The green eyes that possessed a feline sixth sense to see out of the back of his head, had spied her walking down the road, and by the time she reached the gate, he was in flight, a tiny warm, tiger streak that had collided with the speeding car, been tossed into the air and out of life.

The banks of memory broke, releasing a flood that brought with it a sense of drowning, as she leaned against the gate until, taken unawares, she was blinded by the dazzle of an on-coming car's headlights as it swung at speed round the corner. Rage against the whole living, breathing world regenerated strength in her limbs, propelled them into a stumbling run into the middle of the road, her fist holding the torch raised high in the air, words gushing out of her mouth so alien to her ears they must, unbeknown to her, have seeded themselves on her tongue. The car swerved to avoid her, skidded, veered towards the hedge, stopped dead, the driver's head turned, visible under the flare of the torch. Then before she reached it, it reversed, spurted away, the evil little red lights eaten up in the darkness.

*

Edmund was a hundred yards past the junction with Bateman's Lane when the nightmare materialised out of nowhere: a ghost-figure in a moonscape brandishing a fist in the air, mouth agape, seemingly bent on committing suicide under his wheels. For a second the shock numbed him into immobility that was succeeded by a yawning incredulity at a potential havoc let loose in his life.

And she was still pursuing him, hobbling, breaking into spurts of running, a nemesis, a witness to his being where he was. It was the sight of the crazed face in the light from the torch she held tilted upwards, the obscenities she screamed, that provided him with the impetus to re-start the car. A witless old tramp prowling the roads by night. Maybe a gypsy, certainly a drunk. Stamp hard on the memory, obliterate it.

By the time he turned into the by-road leading him home, he had subdued both shock and fright. The aftermath of panic was a mere fluttering of the heart as he drove past the five houses that separated him from his own. In only one, veins of light showed between the drawn curtains. His was the last, more isolated than the others, with a wider stretch of woodland separating him from his neighbour on the left. On the right was undulating farmland, small islands of copse. A blessed emptiness.

He drove into the garage, locked it. Inside the cottage he allowed himself the easement of absorbing through his nerve ends the simple perfection of his home. Aeons of time separated him from the winter afternoon Anna had sat beside him in the psychiatric ward, holding one of his hands between both of hers, coaxing, "Remember how we used to dream of living in the country? Well, I've waved a wand, found you a cottage. Admittedly it's small, needs modernising, but it'll be yours. And we'll be near one another." She unloosed a hand, stroked his hair. "Plus something else. As soon as you're fit Garth has promised you a job in the Anderbridge office."

He twisted his head, hiding his face from her, jeered: "He won't, not when he knows where I am. In a madhouse."

"Shush! As far as he's concerned you're recovering from a breakdown triggered off by the shock of Camilla walking out on you after she'd told you she was pregnant with Keith's child."

He mumbled, "He could find out. Rumours, whispers . . ."

"Stop it. You don't have to crucify yourself. I've told Garth you are in a London clinic. A short spell of recuperation." She scolded him as though he were an intractable child. "Can't you see that, at last, it's come right for us? Me moving out of London, setting up the boutique in a country town, meeting Garth, marrying him. And the cherry on top of the cake is that you two belong to the same profession and, with the company expanding, Garth is shopping around for another chartered surveyor now Kingsbury is retiring." She dropped a kiss on his forehead. "Luck has come our way at last, and I'll take care that it never deserts us again. I've paid the deposit on the cottage, and I'll be responsible for the mortgage payments until you are back at work." She gave him a shake. "Eddie, concentrate, visualise it. A new home, a new job. Out of this morgue. Two men are working on the cottage, one retiling a corner of the roof that leaks, the other painting the inside. They've promised they will be finished in a week. You're a voluntary patient, no one can stop you walking out. So, one week tomorrow, I'll collect you from this hell-hole and drive you home, to your own home."

He remembered the stillness, a curious feeling of stepping out of himself into another being. He remembered the day he became free to create the home that had lain like a matchless but unattainable dream in his imagination. He sighed with deep satisfaction, and set about collecting his tools: a plastic mac, thin as tissue, weightless; a pair of old plimsolls, rubber gloves he sometimes wore when gardening, a Smith & Wesson revolver he'd bought from a sleazy second-hand shop in a corner of East London that, now buried under a block of high rise flats, was untraceable—to murder his stepmother. But Anna, creeping round a door, had caught him slotting in the cartridges, clenched her hands in agony, implored, "They'll hang you. You'll be gone from the world, and without you I'll die."

He wrapped the items in the plastic mac, folded it into a neat parcel, took a pencil torch from a drawer in his desk. Ready now, armed to dispose of an enemy only barely this side of death. He switched off the lights, put his ear close to a panel of the front door to catch any sound of a late dog-walker, and when he was assured of the absolute quality of the silence, set out on the three-mile walk, keeping wherever possible to the grass verges, closing in on the hedges when the moon swam out of the vaporous clouds, spot-lighting the landscape and any insomniac who happened to be abroad.

In Anderbridge High Street he crouched back in a doorway to check there was no prowling police car, no drunk lurching out of nowhere, before he unlocked the gate into the parking yard. Garth's car was there. No light showed in any window. The near-corpse had fallen forward in the chair but the pulse, now barely perceptible, was evidence that the last flicker of life for which, if he'd been capable of praying, he'd have prayed, existed.

With his back to the nine-tenths dead man, he bent low, drew the flaccid hands over his shoulders, heaved, then, draining the last iota of his strength, bent to a crouch, hauled the burden that threatened to bear him to the ground, into the parking yard. With sweat pouring from his skin, powerless to subdue the moans and grunts that broke from his lips, he heaved it into the front passenger seat of Garth's Jaguar. As he closed the door a wash of scarlet, as though blood was bursting from his eyes, blinded him. He stood helpless until the pain in his chest eased and the curtain of red faded. It no longer mattered whether the body was alive or dead; its joints would remain supple for as long as he needed.

He returned to his office, and with the pin-prick of the torch examined it. Not one drip of blood had seeped through the towel to arouse either the curiosity of Mrs. Noakes who cleaned the office from 7:00 to 8:30 weekday mornings, or the suspicions of the police who'd go over it with a microscope.

He allowed the car to free-wheel out of the parking yard into the main street, then was forced, once more, to return and lock the gate. No human in sight; not a footstep rang on the pavement. A small town locked in sleep. Then, terrifyingly, the old hag who'd come within an ace of committing suicide under his wheels materialised in his head. He saw the filthy hand clamped on his shoulder, his flesh defiled by the touch of her greasy locks. A fiend-like creature shaking her fist, threatening him with retribution. Had she seen, memorised the number of the car? Behind the steering wheel his stomach retched, his reflexes so impaired that for the first mile he was only capable of a crawl.

Change the burial ground? By-pass the spot where the crazed old woman had pursued him? Turn his back on a site that had miraculously selected itself? Rejig the design that had materialised clear and precise in his brain? And all for some cretinous old drunk who'd as like as not be sleeping it off in a ditch! His will steadied, renouncing what would be a craven act of weakness, a bowing to defeat. To abandon a grave-site that had the merit of being familiar to him would be madness. Once, on one of his solitary Sunday morning cross-country treks he'd lost his bearings and been astonished to find himself in a clearing that was no more than a hundred yards from the exit from Bateman's Wood, a mere two miles from home.

Outside the five-bar gate was a shallow half-moon of space wide enough to park the car off the road, dowse the side-lights, but which afforded no protection from prowling poachers. That was a risk he could not by-pass. As he donned his protective clothing, changed his shoes, pulled on his gloves, stowed the revolver in his pocket, the phantom pair of balanced scales hung before him. Fifteen minutes' work in exchange for a lifetime of security, ease, against immurement in a prison cell for a quarter of a century! The glitter of the reward beckoned, hardening his confidence. The hauling was less arduous this time. He laid the body below a steep, shelving bank, then, tucking in the ends of the plastic sleeves under his cuffs, wrenched off the linen towel, stowed it in the pocket of the plastic mac, held the gun to the head, fired. The sound was a roaring thunderclap that triggered off the whirling of night-birds, announced itself for what it was, an explosion of death for man or beast. His instinctive reaction was to cover his ears, but when his hands dropped slack to his sides, the silence was unbroken; not a rustle of undergrowth being trodden down by footsteps, no hand bearing down on his shoulder. He grabbed armfuls of tangled bramble and ivy, spread it over the head and body as temporary camouflage, wiped the gun clean of fingerprints, laid it beside the corpse, and even though the out-worn plimsolls would yield no identifiable footprint, he walked backwards, scuffing the carpet of tinder dry leaf-mould.

The click of the latch on the gate, signalling the nearness of the end of his night's work released a stream of euphoria. Murder perfectly timed and executed left him with a sense of omnipotence and something else to which he could not put a name: happiness. His acquaintanceship with it had been so fragmented he did not recognise it.

He took off his shoes, drove in socks to within a mile of Fernwell, ran the car into a dead-end. With his torch he minutely examined the floor for shreds of debris, and, despite his gloves, wiped the steering wheel, the leather surfaces with a duster, then slid out of the car, cleaned off the door latches, put on his shoes and struck off along hard field-paths—rendered impervious to footprints by the drought—that would lead him home.

In the kitchen that had a tiled floor he stripped himself of the plastic mac, shoes, gloves, towel and the revolver, made a pile of them on the draining-board which could be wiped down, all sediment flushed away. His fingers were numb, clumsy. He dropped one of the plastic gloves and had difficulty in retrieving it. There was an odd humming in his head, a dragging lethargy in his limbs. Moving like someone drugged, he stumbled into the sitting-room, fell into a chair and on an instant was asleep.

He woke at five, catapulted out of sleep into a razor-sharp awareness of tasks still to be completed. He padded the gun with the gloves and plimsolls, searched for string. There must be a length somewhere, but he couldn't lay his hands on it, nor on the ball of garden twine. Baulked by a triviality he improvised, bound the parcel with an old tie. He folded the plastic mac round the blood-stained towel, went into the garden to collect some stones to act as weights. But the garden, mostly lawn and shrubs, with a sun-dried sandy soil, offered only small pebbles, and he was reduced to sifting them with his fingers. Back in the kitchen he used the sleeves of the mac to tie it in a bundle, then walked across the dew-laden grass the sun had scorched, savouring the ritual ahead. He raised the cover of the well, held the packages suspended and then let them fall into water he could not see, listening to the ghost-echo of the splash.

"There's no bucket," he'd complained to the builder.

"No, sir. And I'd advise you not to have one. Encourages kids to lark about. Get up to mischief. Two years ago there was a boy of nine drowned in an old disused well over Larksbridge way. You being out all day, no woman around the place, you might fancy having the cover cemented on. There's a lot as does that nowadays, to be on the safe side."

Edmund had promised to consider the suggestion, though he had no intention of having the well covered. The dark tunnel drilled deep into the heart of the earth fascinated him. Finally, because the old man had been so insistent, muttering dark threats that the Council if they chose to exercise authority could order him to cover it, he had reluctantly agreed, but not to the cementing. As though, he mused, there had lain dormant in his sub-conscious the knowledge that one day the well would be his dear accomplice.

"How deep is it?" he'd enquired of the builder.

"No one knows with these old wells. Hundreds of years they've been there. Depthless would be my guess."

Inside the back porch he turned, traced the double-track of footsteps visible in the dew—footsteps that within an hour would be obliterated by the unparalleled heat of this long hot summer. Even the day of the week favoured him: the one on which his laundry and dry cleaning was collected from the porch. He stripped, listed the garments, packed them neatly in the box. His socks, as usual, he rinsed out, hung on the kitchen radiator to dry. Only the final chore remained: to wash the kitchen floor.

*

Exhausted, Violet clawed her way through an eternity until she reached the gate, then the door, leant against it listening to the palpitations that threatened to suffocate her and, when they eased, dragged herself into the sitting-room.

Ashes spilt across the hearth, the fire grey and long dead, ungiving of comfort or hope. Tears dripped down her cheeks in slow-time with intervals between each before they seeped into the collar of her woolly cardigan. Withered flowers someone had brought her, though she could not remember who, had drunk their vase dry. Dust, like mildew, coated every horizontal surface. Biscuit crumbs, half a slice of toast she must have trodden on, were embedded in the rug. As an escape from the deadness of despair she advanced on the corner cupboard, took comfort from the collection of miniature china: doll-size jugs, teapots, mugs, a donkey, a pig, a thatched cottage, each gilded with its place of origin: Scarborough, Cleethorpes, Cromer, Shanklin. Released backward in time she smiled at sands that were forever golden, placid blue seas, the tiny waves edged with lace frills washing between her toes.

Tomorrow, she promised herself, she would rinse each piece of china in cool suds, stand it to drain on a soft duster, her fingers as deft and capable as Dorothea's. The tarnish on the three identical oval silver frames awoke fresh tremors of guilt as she wiped the smeared glass with the elbow of her cardigan. One of Mother, one of Father and a third of two girls in their teens, in wide-brimmed floppy hats, dresses with bows at the throat, new gloves clasped in their hands. Nerves tight as fiddle-strings, at the crucial moment the camera clicked she had sucked in her lower lip, so was preserved for all time as a girl with only half a mouth. Dorothea glared ahead, challenged the camera to do its worst.

The hands on the clock on the mantelpiece pointed to ten minutes to six. But how could that be when it was night, the light she'd switched on burning above her head? Had she slept the night away in the chair? Was it morning? But by six o'clock shouldn't it be daylight? Unless it was winter. No, she remembered distinctly that yesterday, or was it the day before, she'd tripped over a trailing spray of Frau Druska that had been Dorothea's favourite climbing rose. There'd been leaves on it, blooms dropping their petals. So it must be summer, some dark hour buried deep in the night. The clock needed winding, but when she lifted it from the mantel, she discovered with a sense of calamity that it was fully wound. Like the alarm clock upstairs it had ceased to tick when Dorothea's heart died. She pulled up the cuff of her cardigan. Her wrist was bare of one of the identical watches she and Dorothea had given one another. Her top lip trembling, she searched for the watch in every likely and unlikely hiding place before she accepted that the simple act of remembering was no longer automatic but a crazy game she hardly ever won.

The funeral director, a kindly, tactful man, in a muted reverential voice, had queried the gold watch on Dorothea's wrist. Wouldn't she like to keep it?

"Steal it from her! But she'd want to take it with her."

"Of course. I understand."

"And her pearls. We each had a necklace of pearls when we were twenty-one."

"And the pearls." His grave smile was consoling, respectful. "It shall all be as you wish, Miss Madden."

On the landing at the top of the stairs, of their own accord her feet stopped outside the first door. Sometimes she opened it, observed as though it belonged to a lost world, its stripped, stark neatness, hearing Dorothea scolding her for untidiness. "Saves time when you don't have to hunt for things. A place for everything, everything in its place. That's my motto and you'd save a lot of shoe-leather if you learnt it by heart. Lose your head one of these days if you don't watch out."

With Dorothea buried in a grave on the fringe of the churchyard there was no comfort to be gained by opening the door when the room was embalmed in her heart forever.

In her own bedroom the backlog of wasted days was an added weight on her conscience: the eiderdown in a crumpled heap on the floor, dressing-gown sliding off a chair, odd shoes scattered across the floor, a wash-cloth that should have been hanging on the bathroom rail, in a squeezed damp lump on the mahogany chest, and on the bedside table a mug with two sodden tea-bags at the bottom, a Bible with colour pictures inscribed on the fly-leaf: "To Violet on her twelfth birthday, with love from Dorothea."

Like a sickness the sobs thrust their way upward, emerging from her mouth in alternating whimpers and blubbering gasps. She no longer cared whether it was night or day, only to burrow so deep into the darkness that the present made hideous by speeding cars that murdered innocent animals was stifled out of existence. She seized the eiderdown, hung it over her shoulders like a cape, dragged one corner over her head, crawled on to the bed with her shoes on. No one should be expected to live alone, no one in the whole world. God shouldn't allow it.

*

When Audrey, the middle-aged secretary Edmund had inherited from his predecessor, presented him with his morning mail, she self-righteously registered a complaint. "Mr. Lang, I do wish you'd do something about the towels in the visitors' wash-room. I checked there were two clean ones hanging on the rail yesterday afternoon, and now there's only one, and the bin's empty. I'm perfectly aware that these days everyone thinks they're at liberty to make off with anyone else's property,

but to my old-fashioned way of thinking, that's theft, and ste
should be taken to stamp it out."

"Maybe the solution would be to change over to paper
towels."

"Mr. Rampton doesn't care for paper towels, that's why he
insisted on linen." Having reprimanded him, she added, "You
should speak to Mrs. Noakes, at least give her warning that
you're aware the towels are disappearing."

"She's finished cleaning, off the premises before any of the
staff arrive. I haven't seen her for years."

"Then write her a note. Would you like me to draft one for
you?"

"Leave it for the moment. If the towels continue to disappear, I'll pin a notice on the board asking the staff to make sure
they haven't inadvertently taken one home. Meanwhile, we've
a full morning ahead of us. Give me ten minutes to make a telephone call and then bring in your note-book."

She expressed her disapproval by an audible sniff, a toss of
her head. Not firm enough by half, Mr. Lang. Anything for a
quiet life, with a backbone of India-rubber.

But when Edmund lifted the receiver to ask for a private
line, he abruptly changed his mind, cancelled the call. There
came to him a memory of the uncanny empathy that existed
between him and his sister. He recalled odd occasions when simultaneously identical thoughts had surfaced in their minds
and Anna, bursting into laughter, had put them into words.
This eerie talent of hers constituted a faint hazard that he was
not prepared to accept. Not that Garth's death would prostrate
her. She had weathered the divorce remarkably well and with
Garth remarried she could hardly claim widowhood.

He decided he would telephone his sister that evening when
she would be home from one of her tri-annual buying sprees at
the wholesalers from whom she purchased most of her stock for
the boutique.

His immediate task was to assume a mask of normality, be
mildly disturbed but not panicked when Garth failed to turn
up at the Fernwell head office.

Instead he made an internal call. "Johnson, would you come in in about half an hour after I'm through my mail? Mr. Rampton looked in yesterday evening to discuss the Malden Hill property, and I'd like to put you in the picture."

TWO

In the long lost days of her youth Nelia Furston had been accounted a beauty: a willowy blonde with an appealing air of helplessness and fragility that never failed to rouse a protective instinct in males from sixteen to seventy. Now the talent for light-hearted joyousness had been filched from her, leaving her with faded hair, a face that was a network of lines, hundreds of them, as if her skin were a screw of tissue paper that had been scrunched into a ball and carelessly smoothed out. The limitless energy, gaiety of spirit had withered, left in its place an aching spine, a permanent effort to behave as though she hadn't a care in the world, when she was beset by them. As if the golden years in India had exacted a toll for balls that only dawn had quenched, with the ranks of salaaming servants waiting on her bidding.

But, she chided herself, all that beauty and grace was thirty years ago. There had been intervening foreign postings but it was India, that beflowered, scented land, that remained a floodlit backcloth in her imagination.

Standing in the kitchen, hearing the rumbles of thunder, her spirits were at zero level. Four nourishing meals to prepare seven days a week! Like the man in the Greek fable—what was his name?—rolling a boulder endlessly up a hill and never reaching the top. Of course she was delighted to have two grandchildren to stay while their parents were in Hong Kong, though she'd refused point blank to give house-room to the dog, but she'd never visualised the unremitting expenditure of mental and physical energy, the everlasting *thinking*.

Not that Miles was a problem: a sensible, thoughtful boy.

Look how he'd offered to clean the shoes that morning! And so handsome with his indigo eyes and dusky lashes that friends were forever murmuring in her ear, "My, you must be proud of him!"

No, it was Tilly who kept her permanently braced to act as a buffer between granddaughter and grandfather; to damp down before they erupted distressing scenes like the one this morning when Tilly had appeared in a pair of jeans with a hole in one knee, been banished to clothe herself decently in a skirt or dress. To Reggie the sight of a female in trousers was an affront to decency.

Well, Army officers, especially retired Colonels, didn't mince their words. It was unrealistic to expect them to exercise tact when they'd been conditioned over a lifetime to issuing orders, as if, in their hearts, they still lived on a parade ground. Nostalgically, she remembered her only child at Tilly's age: engaging, sweet-natured, with blonde hair that, with a bit of coaxing you could curl round your finger. And what had become of that erstwhile cherub? Carrot hair now, dyed, cropped close to her head, trailing in the dust the shoddy dresses that might have been picked out of a Victorian jumble sale, instead of bought at ridiculously inflated prices. Not that Nelia would have dreamed of breaking her self-imposed edict of forswearing criticism. She vowed she never would, even though her regard for her son-in-law was, to say the least, cool. Young executive type —though he wasn't all that young, in his mid-thirties, with flecks of grey in his long hair that curdled Reggie's scorn, loading her with the task of coddling him back to tranquillity. That was the heart of the strain, keeping Reggie relaxed, holding at bay the bursts of choler that sent his blood pressure racing towards danger level, coaxing him out of the misery and indignity of being dependent on arm crutches.

And, looming over her like a black cloud was what Reggie called "Inspection Day": the three-monthly visit to the London hospital for tests, of being subjected to pricks, probes, X rays. Games, he jeered, easy money for that fool Meredith. Only she knew the rack that stretched his nerves as he waited

for the verdict. Improved? Worse? Stabilised? Her poor darling.
Reduced at sixty-four to what he called an old crock.

With the simple daily routine she'd devised shattered by the
children, she mourned that blissful hour after lunch, when
she'd arrange the cushions to ease the aches in Reggie's bones,
put *The Times* in his hand, know within a minute of her closing the door, he'd nod off, with no one to hear whether or not
he snored. Then she'd climb the stairs, stretch herself on the
bed, and sink into her siesta. A delicious opting out of the
world now outlawed with the children in the house. Tilly, with
her maddening trick of disappearing leaving Nelia at the mercy
of visions of skidding lorries, sleazy men in dirty rain-coats
shadowing an innocent, unsuspecting child down a dark alley.
Then, when her anxiety was near unendurable, appearing,
insisting she'd been in the garden which Nelia, who'd searched
every inch of it twice over, knew to be a lie. Tilly, seemingly incapable of differentiating between truth and fiction; not even
making the effort. All the fault of the modern schools where
children did what they fancied, answered back, never learned
discipline. She sighed with exasperation. Naturally she loved
her only granddaughter, but the tax on her nervous system was
severe.

So, although she had checked an hour ago that Tilly was
reading in her bedroom, conscience drove her to climb to the
third floor and reassure herself that Tilly hadn't disappeared to
goodness knew where.

*

Tilly sat cross-legged on the bed, hugging Kipper, sucking
what remained of his left plush ear. At seven years and ten
months she was under-sized for her age, with stalklike arms and
legs, an ivory-skinned triangular face that was reduced in size
by the jet-black fringe overlapping her eyebrows which she obstinately refused to have trimmed. She'd been late in shedding
her milk teeth and there was a yawning gap where the two
centre ones were no more than a few millimetres of promise
protruding from the pink gums. With hair so fine it tended to

clot in strings over her shoulders, her one redeeming feature was her eyes, grey, lustrous, with whites that dazzled, and long, feathery lashes. Regarding her off-spring, the skin that never acquired a blush of colour, her mother grumbled, "I don't know! You eat like a horse and look as though I kept you tied to a stake in the cellar, fed you on bread and water."

Tilly relinquished Kipper's ear, slid the sheet of white cardboard from under the pillow. Her father's good-bye present, it was divided into twenty-one squares, one figure in each. "You cross out one square when you go to bed, and soon there's none left. That means that Mummy and I will be home, and so will you and Miles."

"And Rufus?"

"And Rufus."

"They won't starve him, chain him up?"

He tapped her nose with two crossed fingers. "I swear. He'll have the same food as he eats at home. Even his bones. I bought them specially from the butcher to put in Mrs. Hunt's deep-freeze."

"But he won't know where he is. He'll think we don't love him any more!"

He hugged her to his side. "Dogs can't count. They eat their heads off, sleep, have races. Mrs. Hunt bred Rufus. She's very proud of him, so she'll take extra care of him. And he'll meet up with his mother, half-brothers, cousins, have romps with them." He gave her a gentle shake. "Honey-bun, I have to go, it's business."

"What sort of business?"

"A process called cost-effectiveness, which means someone from London has to fly out and examine the books, do a lot of sums. Make sure no one is wasting precious time or money. And, Tilly, when the boss says go, you go."

"But Mummy needn't. If she stayed home, we could stay too, and Rufus."

He tweaked her ear. "You selfish little brat. Mummy's earned a holiday from cooking, housework, laundry, looking after us, plus teaching art to a class of moronic students four afternoons a week. She needs a break. You love her more than you love Rufus, don't you?"

"Yes," she lied to please him. Daddy, Rufus, Kipper, Mummy, that was her secret table of love. Miles had been rubbed out. Sucking up to grandfather, offering to run errands for Granny, everlastingly dogging *her* heels, spying on her! Yuck!

Nelia opened the door. "You all right, darling?" And proceeded tactfully to explain that her grandfather loved to see her in a pretty dress and that she must make allowances if he spoke sharply because he was seldom out of pain. Would Tilly try to remember?

Tilly promised. Only half-reassured—you could never tell what the child was thinking—Nelia re-trod the three flights of stairs. And there, in the kitchen was a lovely surprise: Miles peeling the potatoes!

Though it was cheating to mark off the day before bedtime, Tilly crossed it out with a black crayon. That made seven crosses. He'd promised she'd receive a letter when there were four or maybe five. There'd been no letter, only a postcard. That her father had made a promise he hadn't kept was a pain inside her, as though all the woes in the world had collected in a hard knot that would never dissolve.

They were nearly at the end of lunch when Nelia became conscious of a new lightness in the room, a darting sliver of sun that illuminated the bald spot on Reggie's crown. The clouds were flying out of sight, the thunder was silenced. Cautious by nature, she waited ten minutes before she seized the unexpected gift bestowed upon her, beamed winningly at each child. "I've been wondering if you two would like to run an errand for me this afternoon? After being cooped up indoors all morning, it will do you the world of good to taste some fresh air."

Miles, ever accommodating, said, "Of course we will, Granny. What is it?"

Nelia glanced at Tilly, who made no response. A possible setback rose to daunt her, in that she needed both children out of the house, not a stalemate with one in, one out.

"My new dress needs shortening, the cuffs taking up. Miss Galloway does my alterations, and it would be such a help if you'd take her the dress with a note from me. I told her you might be bringing it. She lives on Medway Hill."

Tilly placed her spoon and fork over the remains of the suet pudding she loathed. "I have to wait for the postman."

"Darling, you know very well he never arrives before four. You'd be back in heaps of time."

Colonel Furston's eyes that were like chips of pale-blue ice, fastened menacingly on his granddaughter. "Matilda, your grandmother asked you to run an errand for her. Is that all you have to say?"

Willing to accept any diversion to escape boredom that was fast becoming a permanent state of misery, provided she was back by four, Tilly expressed her willingness to co-operate.

Nelia smiled at the three of them. "That's splendid. In case the thunder comes back, I suggest you set off now while the sun is shining. Play safe, wear your macs. Reggie dear, if you'll excuse me, while the children get ready, I'll collect my dress. I've written Miss Galloway's address on a card, drawn a little sketch map."

Nelia laid the plain postcard on the hall table, followed the outline with her finger. "Down the High Street. When you reach the second set of traffic lights cross over the Fernwell Road, follow it until it joins Medway Hill and on the right you'll see two semi-detached houses. Miss Galloway lives in the first one. And to save you a boring walk over the same ground, you can make a circle. Walk straight on from Miss Galloway's cottage and, on the other side of the road, you'll see a wood with a lane running alongside it. Bateman's Lane it's called. Follow it, and when you turn the last corner you'll be on the main road within sight of home."

"Thanks, Gran. You're jolly clever at drawing maps."

Tilly remembered the weasel. "I know that wood. I went there once with Daddy."

"Did you, darling. Then I'm afraid Daddy took you trespassing. It's private property belonging to Sir Godfry Bilthwaite who keeps pheasants." She gave them each a pat. "So stay in the lane."

As soon as the door closed behind them Miles, ever alert to lay bare one of the unending lies in which his sister excelled, demanded, "When did you go into the wood?"

"Last summer, the day of the wedding anniversary party. Daddy and I took Rufus for a walk because Grandfather went on nagging about Rufus trampling across his flowerbeds."

"Oh, that!"

Behind the closed door, Nelia savoured the bliss. After making Reggie comfy, she'd whisk the dishes into the sink, leave them to soak, and then up the stairs! Miss Galloway, who shared her house with an invalid niece who would otherwise have been doomed to an institution for the chronically disabled, was both compulsively hospitable and garrulous. Favoured with few visitors, she wasn't likely to allow the children to escape before she'd fed them on biscuits and orange squash. To expiate the niggles of guilt, Nelia vowed she'd bake scones for tea.

Srinagar was engraved on a bronze plate screwed to the gate. Tilly, who'd never noticed it until the afternoon they'd taken Rufus for a walk to safeguard the Colonel's flowerbeds, had been baffled by it. "How do you pronounce it?" she asked her father. He told her, explained that it was a lush green town set high on the foothills of the Himalayas in India to which English officers and Embassy officials retreated to keep cool in the punishing heat. And where her grandparents had become engaged.

Now she said the name under her breath in memory of an afternoon of matchless wonder: the three of them walking line abreast, out of range of eyes that ordered her to do this, or don't do that. And the weasel! She brooded. "Granny only wanted to get rid of us, didn't she?"

"I don't blame her. Who'd want you sulking around! You know Grandfather can't stand the sight of girls in trousers!"

Since Miles, to suggest he had no connection with her, chose to walk two steps ahead, she fixed her gaze on his shining gold head, an inch trimmed off the day before they left home to guard against Grandfather having something called apoplexy. Once they'd been tolerant companions, on occasions allies, until that day, a year ago, when blinking to hold the ignominious tears at bay, Miles had been bundled into the car and driven by his father to a boarding school a hundred miles away, exiled from home for three months. He returned thinner, taller, and a stranger, sickeningly polite, opening and shutting doors for his mother, dedicated to cricket and rugger and obsessed by someone called Bywaters with whom he exchanged interminable telephone conversations. One day Tilly had answered the ring and a voice had asked to speak to Allenby. She informed the voice her father wasn't at home. "Allenby Junior, you clot."

Uneasy that a similar fate might lie ahead of her, she pinioned her mother at the kitchen sink. "Will I have to go to boarding school like Miles?"

"Over my dead body!" Lucy Allenby gave her daughter what was supposed to be a merry smile, but was actually a wrath-packed grimace. "That's a fate reserved for small boys. Like lambs to the slaughter, dutifully following in their father's footsteps. A sacred ritual: the same prep school, public school and university. So thank your lucky stars your mother went to eight schools in ten years and you'll come home to sleep in your bed, not in a dormitory with a lot of sadistic little monsters for company."

Saved, Tilly accepted that the new Miles was lost forever.

They bickered all the way to Miss Galloway's door-bell. At the sight of them she clapped her hands in delight. "Mrs. Furston's grandchildren! Oh, what a lovely surprise!" She called over her shoulders, "we'll be with you in a minute, Amy."

Beaming, she stripped them of their macs, shooed them into a fusty, airless sitting-room and introduced them to a skeleton wrapped in rugs in a wheel-chair. Squash and iced buns appeared as Miss Galloway, her head constantly nodding, platitudes streaming from her lips, chattered away while the emaciated woman in the wheel-chair smiled, dribbled and occasionally made little ejaculations. As Tilly could have predicted, the attention of the two women which had been divided equally between the two of them, was soon wholly focused on Miles. How did he like his new school? What games did he play? What were his favourite lessons? Did he get enough to eat?

With courtesy and charm Miles supplied the answers and when three quarters of an hour had elapsed, thanked them for their hospitality, shook two pairs of hands and gave his sister a sharp nudge in the middle of her spine.

Tilly responded with muttered thanks. No power on earth could have propelled her into the arms that were reaching out to her from the wheel-chair with their clawlike purple hands.

Once out of sight of the house, Miss Galloway waving at the window, Miles's contempt spilled over. "You're the limit! A crippled, half-paralysed old woman, stuck for the rest of her life in a wheel-chair, and you didn't even speak to her, acted as if she'd got the plague or something. If you couldn't behave decently, why didn't you stay at home?"

"Srinagar isn't home." She tossed her head. "If she's Miss Galloway's niece, she can't be all that old."

He glared at her. "You're a self-centred brat, an . . ." He choked on a word he couldn't remember, and then miraculously found it on his tongue. "An egomaniac, that's you. A sub-human creep who never thinks about anyone but themselves. Dad would have been ashamed of you. Sucking the ends of your hair. Ugh! Of all the filthy habits!"

She dropped behind to avoid any chance of Miles seeing the rush of tears that misted her eyes. If he'd dropped dead at that moment she'd have walked right over him.

When the gate came in sight, despite her grandmother's strictures, she was powerless to resist the temptation. Miles made a grab for her arm, missed it. "Where do you think you're going?"

"To sit on the gate."

"Can't you read? It says PRIVATE PROPERTY. That means keep out."

"Only inside the gate, not on it." Though there was no padlock on the gate, and she could have opened it, she chose to scramble up, sit on the top bar, surveying the drowsing woodland, remembering that never-to-be-forgotten afternoon.

Miles grabbed a handful of her mac, pulled, but she wheeled about, slapped him hard on each cheek. Startled, his face stinging, he stepped back a pace and then, hands bunched like a boxer's—he was in the initial stages of learning the art at school —came at her.

"Punch me," she screamed, "go on, punch me. Make my nose bleed, give me two black eyes. Go on, I dare you."

It was a dare that chilled Miles's flesh, threatened him with retribution too appalling to contemplate.

"Stop behaving like an ass. Get down, or you'll be arrested for trespassing."

"Make me! Make me!" she challenged.

In the mildest bout of wrestling, she'd not emerge unscathed but with tell-tale bruises, scratches, running blood, evidence that he'd battered his little sister.

Retreat wasn't merely the wisest tactic, it was the only one. Aping nonchalance, he said, "Oh, stop playing the fool. Find your own way home. If you get lost you've only yourself to blame."

He slouched twenty yards up the lane, sat down resignedly in the hedge to wait for Tilly to come to her senses. If she possessed any.

That other summer's day they'd slotted Rufus's lead round the post, swung open the gate, their eyes focused on the unfolding green depths of the wood, as her father named the trees until they merged into a distant blur. The birds, in the heat of the afternoon, were silent except for the blue flash of a jay that heralded its flight with a single squawk.

She pointed. "What's on the other side of that high bank? Rabbits?"

"Could be, but they'd scuttle into their burrows before we had a chance to see their tails."

"Let's explore. Oh, please, Daddy." She tugged at his hand. "Just as far as the bank."

"And run into a gamekeeper armed with a shot-gun! Getting peppered with shot can be painful."

She danced backwards on her toes. "Only as far as the bank. We might see one rabbit that has stayed behind. Oh, please, Daddy." Then, not waiting for permission, she sprinted to the edge of the bank, climbed up until she could lie full length on the slope, peer down into a twilight freckled by pools of sun.

He crouched beside her. "One of these days you'll land me in gaol." He pointed a finger. Chestnut fur, burnished like fire, no more than four or five inches long, it sped with the swiftness of light over the bole of the beech-tree, sniffing in crevices, whisking hither and thither, then freezing, the tiny head uplifted, alert, scenting danger. One of her outflung feet slipped, cracked a twig, and it vanished as though swallowed into the earth beneath it.

"It was so beautiful, so happy . . ."

He hauled her to her feet. "A weasel, a ferocious little beast that given the chance would nip your fingers to the bone." He brushed her clean of soil and leaves. "Come on, back to Rufus. If anyone asks you how you got yourself into such a filthy mess, say you fell down, which is near enough to the truth. Your grandfather has a great regard both for Sir Godfry and the sanctity of private property. Okay?"

"Okay. The weasel was the same colour as Rufus, wasn't he?"

"More or less. What happened to your hair-ribbon?"

"It fell off. Maybe the weasel will take it into his nest. Do weasels have nests?"

"I wouldn't know." He endeavoured to comb her hair with his fingers, failed dismally, and gave up. "Oh, what the hell! You and I will never pass muster, will we?"

"Never," she shrieked, laughing, holding his hand, hearing his laughter mingling with hers. When they untied him, Rufus,

tongue hanging out of his mouth, seemed to be laughing with
them.

That was how the weasel became for Tilly a symbol of un-
blemished joy. She longed for it to be frisking round the bole of
the beech-tree. Like a small, living talisman that would bring
her luck so that when she returned to Srinagar there'd be a letter waiting for her.

She advanced on tiptoe, by-passing twigs that might crack
underfoot, not because she wasted a thought on Sir Godfry's
keeper and his pheasants, but because the weasel was shy, prepared at a tick of sound to dive into oblivion, deprive her of
the joy of watching the glistening, sinuous little body.

Glance downbent, her eye was caught by a bright wink. She
bent, picked up a watch, man-sized, gold, its leather strap broken. She held it to her ear and listened to the satisfying sound
of the measured tick, spat on the glass face, polished it bright
with the hem of her skirt before she tucked her piece of treasure trove into the pocket of her mac and, well-grounded in the
fact that finders weren't necessarily keepers, shelved the little
matter of conscience, and continued her climb up the bank. At
the top she gazed down the falling incline on the far side. Not
even a fleeting glimpse of that frisking red streak. Nothing
stirred over the mammoth tendons of the beech-tree roots.
Nothing alive in sight. Denied her hope, she kicked a clod of
leaves, watched to see where it landed. Ten feet, maybe even
twelve, by someone's old shoe. She began to plot one of the
fantasies she was adept in spinning in her head until it was so
firm and clear she could actually see it. The weasel, in a frenzy
of fussy pride building a nest in an old shoe.

She skidded down the bank into a sultry well of deep
shadow, saw not one shoe but two. The fantasy dissolved.
Imagination could conjure one shoe into a weasel's nest, but
two shoes spelt what Tilly had been taught to regard as a sin:
LITTER. To be collected, taken home and disposed of in the gar-
bage bin, or a hole dug in the garden.

The shoes, she discovered weren't old; they had socks in
them that disappeared into trousers. And through the thick

overhang of bramble and ivy even in the dark shade she glimpsed a small portion of a bloodied face and a shirt collar covered in a brown crust.

Television for children was strictly rationed in the Allenby household. No viewing before you could deliver irrefutable evidence that homework had been completed; text and exercise books packed into a satchel to avoid hysterical wails of them having mysteriously disappeared in the night as Mummy honked at the gate. Meals eaten at a table, not squatting on a rug, blindly poking food into their mouths. One hour per weekday night was Tilly's ration; the selection hers provided the credit titles were rolling by 8:00 P.M.

Tuesday was what her father called cops-and-robbers night. Good cops, bad cops, skidding cars, villains on the run, a high-speed guessing game before the innocent were vindicated, the guilty handcuffed. And always, as some stage, a corpse, plus the accoutrements of murder: a tent, tweezers, cellophane bags, and the public kept at bay by a policeman uttering the time-honoured platitude: "Move along there, please."

Tilly's reaction to instant death was neither shock nor horror; rather an amazed gratification that a scene with which she was familiar on the television screen, was lying three-dimensional and *real* before her eyes. And she'd found it! All by herself.

She clambered up the bank on all fours, pushed open the gate, and began racing up the lane, her duty plain, unstained by a thread of doubt. Miles lunged out of the hedge, tried to grab hold of his fleeing sister, but the slippery macintosh eluded his grasp and she went free.

"What's the panic, where's the fire?" he shouted.

For a second she slowed her pace, yelled over her shoulder. "There's a dead man in the wood." Then she was off, out of sight beyond a curve in the lane.

Sheer fury at the ridiculous melodramas she was forever inventing, the lies she concocted to grab attention, held Miles rooted to the ground, then he began to pound after her but, with less weight to carry than her brother, plus released adrenalin that put wings on her feet, Tilly outdistanced him. When, half choking with righteous indignation, he caught up with her, she was inside a telephone kiosk, speaking into the mouthpiece.

He wrenched open the door, eavesdropped. "Who are you talking to? What game are you playing?"

She ignored him. "Yes, I'll wait by the call-box until you come." She hung up the receiver.

Miles shouted, "How could there be a dead man?"

"There could be because there is."

"You're making it up. Or else you saw something that looked like a dead man but wasn't. Some sort of animal."

How stupid he was! If it had been an animal, she'd still be in the wood, crying because she couldn't bear an animal to die.

She left the kiosk and nonchalantly leant against the door, watching the road for a police car speeding towards her, officers bursting from all four doors. She had to wait five minutes, during which she remained deaf to Miles's alternating threats and pleas.

It was a slight anti-climax that there were only two policemen in the car. One didn't stir from behind the wheel, the other young, blond, with a passing resemblance to Sergeant Drake of Tuesday night, gave her a good-humoured nod. "You the young lady who dialled 999?"

"Yes." She pointed in the direction of the lane. "He's in the wood. I left the gate open. But you won't see him until you're at the top of the bank."

"And he's dead, you say?"

"My sister," Miles implored . . .

The policeman turned to him. "Ah, you were with her, were you, sir?"

Before Miles could get in a word, Tilly announced with withering scorn, "He wasn't even in the wood. He never saw the dead man because he was hiding in the hedge."

"Did you enter the wood, sir?"

"No."

The police constable abandoned him, took out a flap note-book, and to Tilly's gratification followed the time-honoured routine. "Your name and address, Miss?"

She recited it slowly and distinctly, adding, "That's not my real address. It's where my grandparents live."

"And what might their name be?"

Miles got in ahead of her, laying emphasis on his grandfather's military rank.

The constable nodded to indicate it was known to him, checked the time by his watch, snapped the note-book shut, replaced it in his pocket.

"Well, we'd better take a look, hadn't we? Can't leave dead bodies lying around. Tell you what, we'll give you a lift home. Just up the road, isn't it?"

"But I have to come with you. You might not find him."

"Oh, I think we will, Miss. We're very experienced in finding dead bodies. Come on, hop in, both of you. Tell you what, I'll promise to keep you informed of developments." He winked at no one in particular.

She scowled contempt at him. "You think I'm making it up, don't you?"

"She is," Miles said. Then, ashamed of disloyalty in the presence of strangers, added, "She sees things that aren't there. She can't help it."

Tilly sedately folded her hands in her lap. "He's in the wood, at the bottom of a bank, all covered in ivy and stuff, except for his feet."

The constable pressed his foot hard on the accelerator. "Well, we'll soon see, won't we?"

Tilly didn't deign to reply.

Decanted from the car, Miles hissed, "You blithering, half-witted clot! Now the police will come to the house, want to know why you invented a sick joke. Only they won't count it a joke. They'll call it malice, wasting their time, and have you up before a juvenile court. Dad will go berserk."

"No, he won't. You can't say nothing when you find a corpse, *that's* against the law. The police have to find out why he died."

"Oh, dear," Nelia murmured as she saw Tilly. "You do seem to have got yourself muddy. Never mind, it'll wash off." With the lunch dishes disposed of, the scones in the oven, her face "done," she was relaxed, armed to cope with the temporary burden fate had laid upon her. "Go upstairs and tidy yourself for tea. And, Miles dear, your grandfather's finishing off *The Times* cross-word, and he's stuck for three across and four down. I'm sure he'd welcome a little help."

*

At a loss for adequate words to express a revulsion that left Nelia feeling sick, she stared hypnotically at the young police-man sitting stiff and upright in her drawing-room. "I really don't know what to say. An innocent child stumbling . . ." Her voice broke as she struggled to hold back the tears.

"I shouldn't upset yourself, madam. Children of that age are very resilient, and surprisingly tough."

Nelia shuddered. Tilly finding a corpse, not running away screaming in horror, but counting it a triumph, as though she'd won a prize.

The colonel directed a look similar to one he'd awarded many a young subaltern who'd failed in his duty. "A most unpleasant business. Are there likely to be any repercussions as far as my granddaughter is concerned? I assume you have no intention of subjecting a seven-year-old child to police interrogation!"

"Certainly not, sir. But it would be helpful if she could answer one or two questions."

Determined at all costs to avoid direct contact between Tilly —a born exhibitionist—and the police, the colonel rapped out his orders. "In that case, you will address your questions to me. I will put them to my granddaughter and her answers will be conveyed to you in writing."

"The first, sir, how long was she in Bateman's Wood? Ten minutes? Half an hour? Secondly, did she touch the man's clothing? She might, for instance, have laid a hand on his shoes, buttons on his jacket. We're testing for fingerprints, and it is just possible we might have to ask permission to take the young lady's." He cleared his throat. "Superintendent Deacon asked me to say that he would like to have a word with you in the morning, sir."

"Then I suggest he telephones me." The notion that his granddaughter might be fingerprinted like a common criminal he dismissed out of hand.

"She's only a little girl, officer!" Nelia beseeched as though he were about to snatch Tilly from her bed, cast her into a prison cell.

"My dear, we're all aware of that." The colonel glared at the constable. "Suicide or murder?"

"Impossible to say, sir, until after the post-mortem."

"Who was he?"

"When I left the station he hadn't been identified."

The colonel gave him a nod of dismissal. "Thank you, constable. Be kind enough to advise your superiors that if any mention of my granddaughter's name appears in the Press, I shall take appropriate action. Good night to you."

When Nelia returned from showing the constable out, she wailed, "Why didn't she tell us? Why keep it from us? Eating her tea, as though it were a perfectly normal afternoon, three scones and two pieces of cake! And all the while . . . well, what she'd seen!"

The colonel snorted. "No discipline. Never been taught to respect the truth. Spoiled by her father. What can you expect?"

Nelia shook her head distractedly, "But Miles?"

"Different character altogether. School's been the making of him. You won't catch him telling lies, knows better. According to that police fellow, he never entered the wood, committed no act of trespass. He took it for one of Tilly's practical jokes, and with reason. No blame attaches to him. I'll see them both in the morning, and that, my dear, will be the end of this squalid business."

In moments of crisis, Nelia, ever aware of her husband's blood pressure, anxious to keep it from rocketing into a figure that threatened a stroke, tended to adopt the mien of a dutiful

Victorian wife. Nevertheless, she could not resist one plea. "I'd like to go up and see them, make sure both children are all right."

The prim line of his neat snow-white moustache conveyed disapproval. "Very well, if you must," he finally conceded, "but don't on any account be drawn into any discussion. You can't believe a word that child utters."

No streak of light was visible under Tilly's door. Nelia opened it softly, left it open to admit a soft glow from the bulb on the landing.

Tilly was asleep, the semi-bald donkey she called Kipper beside her, the wet ravaged ear lying against her cheek. Her right arm lay on the coverlet, clutching her father's airmail letter from Hong Kong that had come that afternoon. Propped up against the clock on the bedside table was a postcard. Nelia picked it up, took it outside to read under the landing light.

Dear Mistress,

Just to tell you that although I miss you terribly, it's not too bad here. Good grub and plenty of it. Mrs. Hunt took me and Felix—he's my second cousin—for a three-mile run across the fields yesterday afternoon. Of course I get lonely for you and sometimes feel like howling, but Mrs. Hunt's a decent sort and does her best to keep us happy. Every morning she tells me I'll soon be home.

Lots of love and licks,
Rufus.

There followed a double row of kisses.

Nelia propped it against the clock. Obviously from the owner of the kennels. Nelia, untutored in fantasy, found it plain silly pretending a dog could write.

Outside on the landing, a mute pyjamaed figure was lying in wait for her. "Miles, dear, you should be in bed asleep, not standing about in your bare feet."

"I heard the policeman come and I couldn't go to sleep until I knew for certain. Was there a dead man?"

She hustled him back to bed, tucked the sheets in tight. "You mustn't worry, darling. I know it was a nasty shock, but it has nothing to do with you or Tilly. People die every day, but we can't grieve for them all, only for those we love. So . . ."

"There was a dead man in the wood! Tilly wasn't lying?"

"I'm afraid there was." She improvised. "Probably some poor old tramp who'd sat down to have a rest, fallen asleep and died. It was very naughty of Tilly to climb over the gate. Your grandfather is very upset. It means he'll have to write a letter of apology to Sir Godfry."

"What will happen now?"

"Nothing," Nelia retorted firmly. "The police will find out who he is, notify his relatives, and that will be the end of it. Now be a good boy and go to sleep." She kissed his satin-smooth forehead and then, her glance touching the far end of the room where a maze of rail-tracks wove complicated patterns between engines, carriages and trucks, said bracingly, "Think of your beautiful train set, how your grandfather treasured it and looked forward to the day when you would be old enough to appreciate it. And now it is yours. You really are a lucky boy, you know. So go to sleep, darling, and don't worry your head about this afternoon."

"Yes, Granny."

She gave him a second kiss. If only Tilly were as amenable!

As she closed the door, the ignominious tears of mortification squeezed themselves between his lids.

*

The colonel conducted the interrogation of his grandchildren on the lines of a court martial. Statements to be committed to paper, read out to each child and then signed by them.

Miles's examination was simple, straightforward. In that he had not entered the wood he could not be accounted blameworthy. The colonel found it wholly reasonable that he should have assumed his sister was lying.

Tilly was another matter. Her demeanour was one of bright

expectation, devoid of penitence. "Well, what have you to say for yourself?"

"I found a dead man in the wood, and I ran as fast as I could for the police."

He hammered his fist on the table. "You committed an act of trespass, ignored a sign which said that land was private property. Can't you read?"

"Yes."

"Then why were you trespassing in the wood?"

"I wanted to see if I could find the weasel."

The colonel became conscious of a thrumming in his head, an advance signal this his blood pressure was rising. There was only one sensible course to take: short-circuit the wretched, sordid business, get it behind him.

"You disobeyed your grandmother's orders, involved yourself in matters which are no concern of yours or any child of your age. Moreover, you have caused your grandmother a great deal of distress. You should be ashamed of yourself. There are two questions the police have asked me to put to you. In each case I want a truthful answer. Is that understood?"

"Please, couldn't I go to the police station, answer them there?"

"No," he thundered. "Did you touch him? Lay a finger on him?"

She shook her head. The colonel wrote down "No."

"How long were you in the wood?"

To pay him back for not allowing her to go to the police station, she swore she didn't know.

"I thought you possessed a watch."

"It's stopped. Mummy took it to be mended." A memory flashed in her head. She had a watch. A super gold watch. She couldn't think how she'd come to forget it, and was panicked for a moment in case she'd lost it. Then she remembered it was safely tucked in the pocket of her skirt.

The colonel, the tempo of the throbbing in his temples increasing, wrote down her brief statement, read it aloud to her. "You swear you are telling the truth?"

"The whole truth and nothing but the truth," she recited solemnly. "Shouldn't I hold a Bible?"

"No. Sign your name where I have put a cross." When she had done so, his chest heaving, he pointed a finger at the door. When she was safely on the other side of it, he leaned back and closed his eyes.

An hour later Chief Superintendent Deacon telephoned. There were a couple of smeared prints on the shoes. He thought it unlikely they would provide a satisfactory lead, but they couldn't take any chances. This being so, a sergeant would call at the house and take his granddaughter's fingerprints. Yes, he appreciated the colonel found the exercise repugnant, but he would make sure that no distress was caused to the child. They'd make a game of it. Deacon finished on a platitude. The colonel would be the first to realise that, however unpalatable, justice had to be served. And after verification, the child's prints would be destroyed.

"Playing to the gallery, in her element!" the colonel stormed. Nelia gazed in mounting alarm at his face that was rapidly turning the colour of a ripe plum, struggled to decide which would be the better restorative: half a small glass of brandy or a cup of coffee. He spurned both, demanded a double measure of whisky, neat.

THREE

Even before sleep had finally dissolved, Anna was conscious of an all-pervading serenity, like a balm, cleansing mind and body of the cankers of jealousy, loneliness and outrage that over the years had congealed into a private purgatory.

Terrified the peace to which she'd woken might vaporise, she opened her eyes wide and in the functional hotel bedroom braced herself to being tossed back into the crucifying past. But no, the sense of being healed remained.

From the day Garth had strode out of the house into the arms of his baby doll, a silent, scarifying monologue had established itself, like a gramophone playing inside her head. She accused him of baby-snatching, lusting after a child—a stupid, drug-sodden child at that—for his bride. She forecast his professional ruin, the laughing-stock he'd made of himself, all in a spuming flow of crowing malice, while presenting to the world an image of cynical indifference to her husband's re-marriage.

So imperceptibly that she had been barely conscious of it, the screeching monologue had ceased. In its place, like a miracle in which she could not wholly believe, there began to flow between them a gentle, loving dialogue of exquisite tenderness. There were even flickers of time when, turning round, she caught a shadow glimpse of Garth: waiting, offering himself to her. Last night she'd climbed the summit of her dearest hope, a new and lustrous glory had dawned between them. Garth loved her. He always had. He always would.

The tears that gushed down her cheeks were no longer the anguished tears of crucifying misery, but a symbol of their mutual forgiveness of one another. A union of body and spirit.

Dear God, dear heavenly Father, she whispered, Garth was coming back to her, to wrap her in his love. That had been his promise while she slept. She did not question it, seek an explanation. Hadn't she always been endowed with a gift for reaching far out into the unknown, seeing, feeling intuitively what was hidden from other mortals? As children she and Edmund had played at guessing one another's thoughts, extending to its utmost limit a psychic power she possessed—and to a lesser degree Edmund—a vibrant sensation that warmed and solaced two children who had no one but each other.

She lay smiling, eyes closed, listening to the voice caressing her inner ear with a passion of love equal to her own. She felt Garth's arms about her as her hands enclosed his face. He was coming home. That was the message he beamed into her heart. The black years of misery were at an end. Home to her, casting the half-witted, gold-digging child-bride clean out of his life.

She thrust her feet out of bed, reached for her slippers and was struck by a whiplash of reality at the sight of herself in the full-length mirror screwed to the wall. Her hand flew to her mouth to stifle the half-cry, half-moan at the hideous sight that confronted her. Tousled black-grey hair, blurred, puffy eyes, arms that bulged above the elbows, splayed, calloused feet. Defying her body to defeat her, she tore off the nightdress, challenged her eyes to accept the naked woman in the mirror. Defiantly she tilted her chin to reduce the sag of her neck; no hollows now, and only the faintest drag to her heavy breasts. She sucked in her breath, held it, but her stomach still bulged, and the flesh on the inner sides of her thighs was wrinkled and flabby.

She raged against the disfigurements inflicted by time. Then, gradually, the night's vision re-asserted itself, dragged her back from the abyss of despair. Garth didn't hunger after a skinny kid—that's what he was escaping from—the brainless adolescent who'd tricked him into marriage. Love wasn't compounded of nymphs and shepherds but of endurance, faith, forgiveness, self-knowledge, depths of passion of which that child-simpleton hadn't a clue. She grimaced into the mirror.

Minor imperfections, nothing that a masseuse, hairdresser, cosmetician, chiropodist couldn't magic away.

She stuffed the limp nylon nightdress with its bunches of bedraggled rosebuds into the wastepaper basket, picked up the cotton dressing-gown and pitched it under the bed. Clothes! Day clothes, evening clothes, night clothes. Appointments that slotted into one another, not a second of time squandered. Telephone Herman—he'd be in his office by 8:30—say sorry she couldn't make the dress-show. He'd splutter fury, but who cared! She'd sweeten him by ordering blind five of his new season's two-pieces. Colours of his choice, the only stipulation that they were sizes thirty-eight to forty-two. The matrons of Anderbridge tended towards wide hips, generous busts, though cunning pinning of display models underplayed that unglamorous fact. The skinny teenagers and early twenties never as much as flicked an eyelid at Annabel's window, but squandered the contents of their bottomless purses on the shoddy clothes in what was called "The Tat Shop" at the end of the street. Carol among them. Anna seeing her emerging from it one day with an armful of plastic bags, had slid into the doorway of the boutique. Not that Carol, who at eighteen was already a man-stealer, a man-mesmeriser, would have noticed her. In her cowboy boots, she drifted along the street like a sleep-walker, the insipid face half-buried under a crimped red wig. How could Garth bear to touch her—she wasn't even clean!

Over her breakfast of two cups of instant coffee, Anna made a list, divided it into sub-sections. On the telephone her voice was tuned to a cajoling note as she requested, not demanded, appointments from half a dozen receptionists who insisted they were booked solid for a week. Her normal hectoring approach was replaced by one of silken charm with an overlay of authority to convey she was a woman unaccustomed to having her wishes thwarted. To Herman's growling, she chided with good-humour. "Now, Hermie, you know the show is a re-run of your spring collection. And why not! It was a winner. The customers lapped it up. Yes, five. I'll be at your next show. Promise!"

With the parking problems in the West End, she left her car

at the hotel, called a cab. The commissionaire, opening the door, received the handsome tip she slid into his palm with a smart salute, a deferential, "Have a good day, madam."

Not only physically reshaped but remade in spirit: gracious, irresistible, with ten years lopped off her age. She emerged from a day of organised frenzy so topped up by elation that she was unconscious of fatigue as she listened to that tender, coaxing voice urging her to hurry home.

She drove the thirty-five miles with the skill and panache of a racing driver, absolved from the tedium of adhering to speed regulations, safeguarded against accidents. Made immortal! Unashamedly she indulged in a cliché: Written in the Stars. A union that no force on earth could dissolve.

As she stepped out of the car she could hear the telephone ringing. She stood irresolute—Garth? Their meeting was so precisely etched into a time and a setting that to transfer it into a different one momentarily confused her. In the end the caller's persistence exerted a compulsion that sent her running to the front door, fumbling to slot the key into its lock.

The ringing ceased the second she crossed the threshold, enveloping her in silence. She sighed relief. She needed time, not much, about an hour, to prepare herself for what she saw as the fulfilment of last night's vision, but with the passion fiercer, till it reached a height that could no longer be borne, and subsided into gentleness, a communion of the flesh.

With renewed pride she examined the room that had once been a source of joy to her—and would be again, no, was again, and was thankful for Garth's foresight in refusing to sell the house that wasn't Carol's style. No picture windows! No swimming pool! Garth had said Anna could keep it for her lifetime, or if she did not choose to live there, it could be leased, the rent paid to her. If he outlived her, the title deeds would revert to him: if he was deceased, to his wife and heirs. That was a laugh: a middle-aged Baby Carol mistress of a rambling Georgian rectory in which no vicar had been able to afford to live for half a century! Carol, at any age, would have been buried in squalor within a month—no respecting cleaning woman would

have worked for her or any of her gang of long-haired drop-
outs.

She checked that her daily help had laid the logs in the
wrought-iron fire basket in the L-shaped sitting-room, put a
match to them and bore her treasure of tissue-lined carrier
bags, dress-boxes, packages of shoes to a spare bedroom. First
thing in the morning she'd empty her wardrobes of clothes, bundle them up and deliver them to the charity shop in the High
Street.

Like a child attacking a mountain of presents under a Christ-
mas tree, she tore at the wrappings until her hands caressed
and held aloft a blush-pink robe of quilted satin, with a tiny
stand-up collar, nipped in at the waist, a fluted swirling skirt—
as regal as a wedding dress. She made a heap of the diaphanous
underwear, the gossamer tights, ran her fingers through them
before she switched to the dress-boxes, spread out on the bed,
the Yves Saint Laurent oatmeal coat and dress, with matching
russet shoes and scarf. Softly she clapped her hands in wonder-
ment: kitted out like a bride, which was what she was.

Meanwhile, she must turn her attention to the three-quarter
empty deep-freeze, make a list of Garth's favourite foods to be
ordered and delivered in the morning. There was the four-
posted bed to be stripped, remade with handkerchief-fine Irish
linen. And flowers—she did a pirouette—perfumed bouquets,
some bought, some picked from the garden but not enough to
despoil it. The silver to be stripped of its green baize wrappings, checked for smears, any evidence of tarnish. Baby Carol
hadn't fancied her hideous modern house littered with dreary
old silver, so Garth, wisely, had left it in her care.

But first, to celebrate, she'd have a drink. Though she'd not
eaten all day, she was no more conscious of hunger than she
was of doubt, as though the certainty that Garth would walk
through the door within an hour had freed her of the mundane
need for food.

Watching the flames curling through the logs, sipping the
martini, she glanced across the room into the gilded mirror on
the opposite wall, smiled at the image of herself. A serene

woman infused by inner radiance, a private sun of happiness, thirty-fivish, maybe younger, with dark hair in which not a sprinkle of grey was visible, so expertly cut and set that each strand fell naturally into a shape that was a perfect frame for her face.

While she sipped, she toyed with the idea of selling the dress shop, disencumbering herself of its responsibility now that she and Garth were to be reunited. Anthea, her first assistant, would jump at the chance of buying it, provided the bank considered her credit-worthy for a mortgage. Well, Garth would handle that, stand guarantor. He was clever with money, never miserly, but equally never wasteful of the not inconsiderable wealth he'd inherited from his father.

She was rinsing her martini glass when the phone rang.

"Thank God!" Edmund's voice cracked in her ear. "I've been trying to reach you for hours!"

"Well, I'm home now." In no mood to have the lovely, loving dialogue interrupted, she added, "I've had a gruelling day, not a moment to get my breath. Be an angel and telephone me in the morning."

"I'll be 'round."

The abruptness with which he hung up jarred—reminding her of the nerve-storms that had overwhelmed, half-destroyed him in his youth. But he'd outgrown them years ago. He was a success in his job; Garth valued his efficiency. His future was secure, and he doted on the old cottage he'd transformed into a small elegant nest for himself. So what was bugging him? For once she couldn't hazard a guess. The likeliest explanation was that a property deal he'd been certain of pulling off had collapsed, or someone had made a casual remark at which he'd taken offence—which he was overquick to do. Well, with a life-time's experience of soothing him, she'd soon sort out any problem that was harassing him. Even so, she was not prepared to spend longer than half an hour on him, not tonight when she knew the precise time of Garth's arrival: 9:00 o'clock, dusk enclosing the house, the long night ahead of them.

She ran upstairs as lightly as a girl, changed into the blush-pink robe, combed a disarranged curl, sprayed perfume on her throat, smiled at the new-born self smiling back at her in the mirror. Then, suddenly, inexplicably, her vision darkened, and there leapt at her the shadow-images of two tortured, terrified children.

She'd been eleven, Edmund ten, when their frail, ever-ailing mother died. The day after the funeral their father had ushered into the house a brassy-haired, buxom woman with a raucous laugh. Mrs. Whetstone, he explained, was to be their house-keeper, take good care of them. In his presence she beamed on them, suggested treats they could expect, which never materialised. When their father was out of the house she subjected them to senseless petty cruelties, viciously denying them any wish they expressed.

It was Mrs. Whetstone, whom their father married within six months, who'd forged the bond of loathing and terror between brother and sister. In the night, crouched on the landing, they listened to the cackling giggles. When their father died, he bequeathed his house, his money, except for five hundred pounds to each child, then aged fifteen and sixteen, to his wife. Two days after the will was read, she'd swept them out of the house as though they were clods of filth.

So, she explained to Garth, I must be patient, listen, give Edmund time to spit out the venom, the putrescence of hate that sometimes, even now, boiled over. Like the day he had wrapped his hands in a stranglehold 'round their stepmother's throat, for which his father had thrashed him until the blood spurted, left weals that had taken months to heal.

She floated into the drawing-room, threw another log on the fire, put out the whisky decanter, soda and a glass to have a drink ready to Edmund's hand as soon as he appeared. Simultaneously she heard the sound of the car spurting up the drive, the slam of a door, his racing strides over the gravel.

She called out to him. "Hi, what's the panic?"

Then, as he walked deeper into the room, her eyes registered his ashen, sweat-dampened face, the dark hair, usually so immaculate, tumbled, his chest heaving with breath that he expelled audibly.

She drew him to a chair, poured his drink and pressed it between his palms, calling him by his childhood name. "Eddy, love, what in heaven's name is the matter?"

He bowed his head, took a deep swallow of the whisky, then with agonising slowness lifted his glance. "Garth . . ."

As the seconds ticked away, she could hear her heart-beats begin to race, feel her new-found joy foundering under a tumult of erupting fear. "What about him?"

"Anna, he's dead."

The words made no impact, just bounced off her.

"Anna," he choked, "you had to be told. There was no way of sparing you. Anna . . ."

She shouted him down. "He can't be."

His gaze was stricken, haunted. "His body was found in Bateman's Wood this afternoon, about four o'clock, by a child."

"What child?"

He couldn't understand why the name of the child should concern either of them. Then he saw her face, dead-white flesh frozen on the bones. In that it was something he hadn't expected, it panicked him. The divorce was over two years behind her, so why should she be so mortally hurt? Shock, yes; grief, yes; tears of course, he had been prepared for all such reactions, but not this. His own shock was severe enough. He could not have foreseen that Garth's body would be discovered within hours. In his mind he had seen it reduced to rot and mould that when found would be barely identifiable as human.

She shouted, "What child?" and he saw the spume of froth on her lips.

"Just a child who reported a body in Bateman's Wood to the police."

"Where did he die?"

"I told you, in Bateman's Wood."

"How did he die?"

He moistened his lips. "He was shot."

Her hands reached out, grabbed his lapels. "Who shot him? Who?"

With an enormous effort, he managed to temper his voice to a plea for reason. "Anna, it's only four hours since the police found him. They don't know."

Suddenly she clamped her hand to her mouth, lurched out of the room into the downstairs cloak-room. With an empty stomach she retched until every inch of her body was sore, its organs strained out of shape. She poured cold water into her hands, sluiced her face, lifted her head and stared into the mirror. The water had soaked her hair reducing it to black strings that clung to her jawbone. Her numbed legs demanded she sit down on the stool while she fought for calm. The leaden minutes ticked slowly by before the truth wrote itself in huge phosphorous letters that dazzled her eyes. Garth had come back to her not in life but in death. For weeks he'd been telling her that he was going to die. Their reunion was to be not of the flesh but of the spirit. Dear God, she whispered, and did not know how she would bear it. She hugged her arms across her breasts, fumbled haltingly towards a second truth. Death which she'd counted the end of life, was not so. Bodies died, but the spirit remained alive. That was why Garth had come to her in the night, why he was with her now.

She hauled herself upstairs, changed into a jersey and skirt, threw a black cloak over her shoulders.

Edmund, pacing the floor, had his back to her when she shouted hoarsely, "Where is he?"

His eyes blinked in disbelief at the transformation in her. When he'd arrived she'd been wearing an expensive dressing-gown, hair satiny with flying tendrils. Now, her hair was in rat's tails, her lips colourless, her skin wrinkled and grey. A tweed skirt was rucked above her knees, her blouse was unbuttoned and she was wearing a pair of old, muddied garden shoes. She looked demented. When with concern he reached for her hand, she snatched it out of his reach. "Where is he?"

"In the mortuary at Fernwell." He hesitated, then plunged on because she had to know. "We had difficulty in contacting

Carol. She left yesterday to stay with her parents, and in the general chaos no one could recall their address, even their name. Fortunately, the woman next door remembered it was Coombes. I had to break the news to Carol over the telephone. She collapsed. Thank goodness she is with her parents. There's some anxiety about the baby, that she might lose it."

The last sentence made no impact on her for the reason she didn't choose to hear it. She swung on her heel. "I'm going to him."

Appalled, he beseeched, "Anna, that's not possible."

"Why not?"

"You haven't the legal right, not any more. With Carol away, the police asked me to identify him. It was Garth."

She swung on her heel. "Your car is blocking mine. Move it out of the way."

He had to run to catch up with her. "Anna, please listen. The police won't allow you to see Garth. In any case it would distress you beyond bearing. Please."

She did not heed him but pulled back the garage doors, climbed into the car, jammed the key into the ignition.

He backed his car out of the way, went towards her. "All right, I'll drive you. But I warn you . . ." As he put his hand on the door, she switched on the ignition, yelled, "I've a right to see him. No one's going to stop me."

She trod so hard on the accelerator that he had to jump back, flatten himself against the wall.

He shouted her name, but she did not choose to hear him as she roared through the gate, intent on a mission she was not prepared to share with anyone: vengeance.

FOUR

Having settled her husband in the hired car that was to drive them to the hospital, Nelia dashed back to the porch where Mrs. Baker, returned from two weeks' seaside holiday, was flanked by Miles and Tilly, conscious of a last-minute message that had flown off the tip of her tongue.

"Have you forgotten something, Granny?" Miles enquired helpfully. "Can I fetch it?"

"No, dear." Her memory obstinately stayed blank. "I just wanted to remind Mrs. Baker to pre-heat the oven before she puts the shepherd's pie in."

Mrs. Baker sniffed, not taking kindly to being instructed in elementary cookery. It wasn't as though Mrs. Furston was much of a hand at it. The shepherd's pie looked a soggy mess to her. She said in her spikiest voice, "Maybe I'd better promise I won't put the trifle in the oven by mistake!"

Though she'd already kissed her grandchildren good-bye, Nelia embraced them a second time, hovered, though Reggie, patience exhausted, longing to have the humiliations of the day, and its verdict, behind him, ordered the chauffeur to honk. Then, as she lowered her foot over the first step, she remembered what she must impress on Tilly's scatter-brained mind.

"Tilly, you're to promise me, on your honour, that you won't go wandering off on your own, worrying Mrs. Baker."

"Yes, Granny, I promise." In that Tilly always intended to keep her promises, her conscience was clear.

Like an old mother-hen, Mrs. Baker thought cynically: that's what came of having only one ewe-lamb of her own! "Don't

you fret." She challenged each child in turn. "Good as gold
you'll be, won't you?"

"Yes," they carolled in unison as three hands waved Nelia
off.

Miles tucked his arm into Mrs. Baker's, bestowed upon her
his most winning smile. She eyed him with mock severity.
"What's the favour?"

"We won't have to eat that shepherd's pie, will we?"

"Shepherd's pie makes me sick." Tilly gave a realistic demon-
stration of her reaction to the food provided.

"Nothing else on the menu. Fish pie for you and her for supper. Dover sole for him. What did you fancy?"

"Fish and chips," they choroused.

"You need money to buy them. Where's it coming from?
Who's going to pay?" Mrs. Baker had no intention of financing
lunch for three.

Miles offered, "I'll pay for yours and mine." He rounded on
his sister. "And you'll jolly well pay for your own."

Tilly, enraged, shouted back, "You're a meanie. You've got
heaps of money hoarded in your tin cash-box. Besides, gentle-
men always pay for ladies."

"You're not a lady, just a greedy kid. You still owe me ten
pence for that ice-cream cornet."

"I paid you back. You've forgotten."

"Settle it between you." Mrs. Baker turned her back on
them. "Provided one of you comes up with the money, you can
slip round to the fish and chip bar, else we'll make do with the
shepherd's pie. Suit yourselves."

The ground cut from under her feet, Tilly went upstairs,
counted out the cost of one portion of fish and chips, handed it
over to Mrs. Baker, who checked it, entrusted it to Miles. "Off
you go, then you won't have to queue. It'll keep warm in the
oven, and I'll put half the shepherd's pie down the loo, so your
poor old gran's pride won't get a bashing. We can't all be fancy
cooks, especially if you've been waited on by an army of darkie
servants. My, that must be the life! I wouldn't say no to having
a blackamoor slave to do my chores."

*

Replete, Mrs. Baker moved her chair back from the table, scrutinised her ankles, pressing them gingerly to test the swelling. Puffy, but less so than they'd been yesterday. Even so, she decided to put them up for an hour.

"What are you two going to do with yourselves this after-noon, that is after you've helped me with the washing-up?"

"I want to mend the broken coupling on my Flying Scot. It upsets Grandfather when it doesn't run, and then he loses his breath."

"Peppery old gentleman. That high colour's not a healthy sign. He'd do well to watch his temper or he'll be taken off like my sister's husband. Swallowing the last slice of his Yorkshire pudding he was, when the fork dropped from his hand, and he was a goner. Mind you, it's the best way to go, even though our Edie has never been the same since. Broods, she does. There are days when you can't get a word out of her."

Tilly burst out, "I found a dead man the day before yester-day. When I was looking for the weasel. A goner," she added, picking up Mrs. Baker's word.

"Did you!" Mrs. Baker had been subjected to two lectures that morning. One from Mrs. Furston, one from the colonel. The substance of Mrs. Furston's was that she was on no account to encourage Tilly to dwell on the dead man discovered in the wood. The less said the sooner Tilly would forget about it.

The colonel had demanded that she take an oath that she would not allow the word corpse—which exerted a morbid fas-cination on Tilly—to pass her lips. If Tilly raised the subject, she was to ignore it. "No comment, that is the line you are to take. You understand what no comment means, Mrs. Baker?"

As if she'd never looked at the telly! She granted him a curt yes, omitting the "sir" he expected. Not that his "no com-ment" would have any effect. People wouldn't stop talking about the Rampton murder, and there were splash headlines about it in the newspapers.

Ignoring Tilly's claim to fame, she demanded, "And what do you propose to do with yourself?"

Frustrated at being denied the satisfaction of minutely reporting her find of a corpse in the wood, all the assistance she'd given the police, having her fingerprints taken, Tilly sulked. "Write my letters to Daddy and to Rufus."

Miles collapsed over the table in a paroxysm of mock derision. "Rufus is a dog. She's writing a postcard to a dog! She believes it can read." He exploded into hoots of laughter.

Tilly glared. "Mrs. Hunt reads it to him. And dogs know more than you do." She lunged across the table to grab his ear lobes.

Miles ducked, Mrs. Baker remonstrated. "Manners, manners! On your feet, both of you."

Tilly whined, "Granny never makes us wash-up."

"That's her business. When you're with her, you do what she says. When I'm here, you do what I say. Now who's going to wash?"

"I am." Tilly leapt up, knowing from experience at home, where they were both expected to help with the chores, that Miles loathed having to handle that most demeaning of all badges of servitude, a tea-cloth.

*

It took Tilly an hour to write the letter to her father and the postcard picture of an old English sheepdog for Rufus, which she addressed c/o Mrs. Hunt. Biting dents in the ball-point pen, she deliberated whether or not she should tell her father about finding the dead man in the wood. There was a risk that Mummy might snatch the letter from him before he'd had time to read it. Intuition warned her that might trigger off unfortunate repercussions. Her mother was a coward. At the sight of a mouse she screamed, jumped on a chair and bound her skirt round her knees. A worm and she looked up at the sky pretending it wasn't there. Blood running from a cut knee and she shook all over, her face turning the colour of uncooked dough. A dead man, Tilly knew for sure, would bring a scream of horror from her mother's lips. Maybe she'd even have a fit! For which she'd be blamed.

Though it required considerable self-denial, she decided to save up the most exciting thing that had ever happened to her until Daddy was home. Anyway, by that time the police might have caught the murderer, and she'd be called as a witness.

She saw herself in the dock, her hand on a Bible, repeating the oath the clerk of the court recited, and down in the well her father's proud uplifted gaze. Reluctantly she limited herself to a hint of the drama ahead. "I've got the most super surprise for you when you get home. The most terrific ever."

She sealed the envelope, re-read the postcard to Rufus. "I know you miss me as much as I miss you, but there are only sixteen more days. For a home-coming present I'll buy you some chocolate drops, the ones you like, not the dog ones. Remind Mrs. Hunt to keep your water-bowl filled so you don't get thirsty. The first day we're home, Daddy and I will take you down to the river for a swim." It closed with three packed lines of kisses.

Upstairs Miles was fiddling with his train set. Downstairs Mrs. Baker, having provided herself with a nest of feather cushions pilfered from a second sofa and a couple of chairs, was snoring decorously. She'd removed her shoes which lay like misshapen boats on the Indian carpet.

Tilly was fascinated by a face that was powerless to stare back at her. It was like being invisible, or spying through a window. Mrs. Baker's cheeks were mottled with a network of tiny bright veins. There was a lumpy blob on the end of her nose, and in the short interlude of silence between each snore her top set of dentures parted company from her gums. Her ankles were thick and there were funny-shaped knobs on her feet.

Tilly tiptoed out and dutifully printed a message on a scrap of paper torn from a pad in the kitchen. "Have gone to post my letters." She signed it Matilda Allenby, laid it on the dead centre of Mrs. Baker's protruding stomach.

Her father having pre-stamped the air-mail envelope, she only had to buy a stamp for Rufus's card. As she dropped them into the lip of the pillar-box the corners of her eyes began to sting. But by the time she was half-way down the High Street the prickling behind her lids was forgotten. The sun was shining, Tilly, clad in her favourite garments, frayed jeans, T-shirt, a pair of sneakers with a hole in one toe, was at peace physically and mentally, minding her own business, mercifully released from the chains of authority, free! She paused at the Sweet-Box to examine the window display. Caramels were 10 pence a quarter. The silky sweetness surfaced on her tongue as she anticipated the well-masticated goo welding her teeth together and then being wrenched apart with a delicious squelching sound. At home caramels, which by suction had removed three fillings from her teeth, were forbidden. She counted out her money. Fifteen pence. She had half-opened the door when she remembered Hudson's supermarket specialised in Bargain Offers. Suppose today's bargain was the rack of pre-packed sweets that lined the check-out counter!

She strolled up and down the aisles, lingering only at the cakes before she joined the check-out, peered round the arm of the woman directly ahead of her, pinpointed the caramels. Eight ounces for 15 pence! She snatched her prize from the rack and holding the money ready to hand to the check-out girl, contemplated the bliss ahead.

Two bumper trolleys emptied, leaving only one customer ahead with a mere three items lying in the bottom of a basket. Tilly was almost there when the woman dropped her purse and a cascade of assorted coins rolled themselves into corners and crevices.

"Beryl," the girl at the check-out yelled. "Give this lady a hand. She's dropped her purse." She smiled comfortingly at the customer. "Not to worry, love, we'll pick it up. Don't you upset yourself."

"I'm so sorry. How silly of me . . ."

"Beryl, there's another 5p over there, and that's about the lot." Beryl put the coins in the purse, and as an extra grace packed the three items in the woman's shopping bag.

"Thank you . . . thank you. How kind . . . thank you."

It wasn't until Tilly was through the check-out that she saw the 50p piece gleaming against the toe of her shoe. She did a lightning dip, scooped it up, put it in her pocket, sauntered out. It could be anybody's. How could you find the owner of a single 50p when there were hundreds of customers passing through the check-out dropping their change every day! Determinedly she blanked out her father's face, and began walking at a fast pace along the High Street until, one caramel lodged comfortingly between her back teeth, she saw directly ahead of her the bright magenta crocheted bonnet of the woman who'd dropped her purse.

Even Tilly, totally devoid of regard for any co-ordination in clothes, could not be unaware of her general dishevelment. Limp strands of mottled grey and white hair had escaped the magenta bonnet, were dripping over her shoulders. She wore heelless carpet slippers, a tweed coat that was half-slipping off her shoulders, a multi-coloured dress that sagged at the back until it swept the pavement, and hanging from her left hand one handle of a plastic shopping bag, that threatened to tip the items it contained on to the pavement.

Conscience pricking, Tilly trailed the figure ahead, allowing herself the luxury of not deciding, when suddenly the woman stopped dead in her tracks, swivelled round and, for the first time Tilly saw her face. Old, all squeezed up except for a mouth that was trembling, with a solitary tear sliding out of the corner of one eye, for all the world as though she'd lost something.

Of its own accord Tilly's fist flew open as she displayed the 50p piece. "You dropped this. I found it on the floor at Hudson's."

The old lady distractedly wiped a few white rat-tails out of her eyes. "Did I?" She shook her head, staring bemusedly at the coin. "I'm afraid I don't remember. Are you sure it's mine?"

"Of course I am. I saw you drop it." In a blaze of virtue Tilly smiled, lied for good measure. "I've been running to catch you up."

The old lady lifted it from Tilly's outstretched palm. "You are a kind little girl. You see . . ." A haze of confusion enveloped her. "I was on my way home . . . at least . . ." She gazed about her, not quite sure where she was even though some of the buildings appeared familiar. Wasn't that the fish-shop on the other side of the road where she used to buy Sammy's cod-pieces?

"Where do you live? Is it far?"

"Medway Hill. The Tied Cottage . . . or is that where we used to live? No, how silly of me, it's where I live now."

"I'll come with you and carry your bag," Tilly offered, the compulsive sleuth instinct rising in her like yeast. "It's on my way home." Well, it was, if you took the long way round. She unwound the one handle from the old lady's hand, slung both straps over her arm. Medway Hill ran parallel to the wood. She'd be able to hang over the gate: maybe find a policeman still on guard at the scene of the crime. Or, best of all, see the weasel.

Once out of the house, cast adrift in streets, subjected to distracting sounds she couldn't identify, the raking gaze of strangers, Violet Madden found the double burden of listening and talking beyond her. Eyes downcast she pattered as fast as her slip-slopping carpet slippers and arthritic knee would permit, driven by a yearning to be safe inside the walls of home, reassure herself that it was inviolate, undisturbed by prying strangers. Even if she didn't answer the door-bell, they flattened their faces against the window-panes, mimed, or if she'd forgotten to lock the back door, opened it and shouted, "Miss Madden, are you there?" and searched the house until they'd found her.

Then, run to earth, cornered, she'd be subjected to the harassment of an inquisition. Was she feeding herself adequately; was she sure she could cope alone? Wouldn't it be a sensible idea if she took advantage of Meals on Wheels? Brought to her door for a minimal charge, less than it would cost to cook her own? The social worker, earnest, hatted, and *au fait* with every amenity in the rule book available to the old, especially those who lived alone, wheedled: "We all know what a chore it is to cook for one. Nibbling is so much easier, but that only stores up trouble. We all need our vitamins otherwise our health deteriorates. What about it? Shall I put you down on our list?"

Violet shook her head, stubbornly refusing to be cajoled or coerced into accepting favours. She also declined to have her dirty laundry collected, thrown into a machine and delivered back to her ready to iron, or have her pension cashed for her. A league of interfering do-gooders, dispensers of charity whom Dorothea had taught her to scorn.

Like the two impertinent brash young men who assumed that now she was alone she'd want to sell Dorothea's car in which they'd been on outings and always, on each of their birthdays, driven to the sea for a picnic. The car, dust-sheeted in the garage, would remain there as long as she lived.

The social worker's eyes discreetly examined the room. "I see you have a radio. Do you keep a spare battery in hand? It's always a good idea."

"Yes," Violet said, though the battery had been dead for months.

"No television? They can be good company."

"No." They'd been saving up for it, the television not to be bought until the money was upstairs in a tin savings box. "Cheaper that way," Dorothea explained. "They make you pay extortionate interest on every penny you borrow."

The woman had smiled at her, but Violet hadn't smiled back. "Please remember that you have friends, Miss Madden. We're trained to sort out any problems you run into, make life easier and more comfortable for you." Violet had promised to remember and shown her the door.

She unlocked it now and was startled when she turned to shut the world out to find a child on her heels.

Tilly, itching with curiosity, announced, "I'll carry your shopping inside for you."

Violet had forgotten her existence, though she retained a blurred memory of the 50-pence piece. Youths, teen-age girls with their trumpet blasts of laughter—lay-abouts, thugs, drug-fiends Dorothea had labelled them—frightened her. But this child was small, a spindly little creature, shorter even than herself, who slipped eel-like into the sitting-room and when Violet followed, was gazing rapturously at a chocolate cake someone had baked for her—not that she could remember who.

"Oh, what a super cake! If only we had some candles we could stick them in the icing, pretend it was a birthday. Have you got any candles?"

Violet shook her head. The very idea of candles evoked sweet but blurred pictures of the past.

"I'm sorry," she blurted out, "but I don't know who you are."

Tilly grinned. "Oh, yes you do. I found your fifty-pence piece. You can't have forgotten. And I carried your shopping bag home. I'm Matilda Catherine Allenby. You can call me Tilly. Most people do, except my grandfather."

"Tilly?"

"Yes. What's your name?"

"Violet Madden."

Tilly's glance flew back to the table. "Aren't you going to cut the cake?"

"Yes." Violet struggled to decide where it could have come from, still holding at bay that word that Dorothea could not stomach: Charity. Never be beholden to anyone, she'd preached sternly. Stand on your own two feet. But surely, if she couldn't remember, the obligation to be grateful didn't exist. And anyway, the little girl was hungry.

Violet, still hatted and coated, disappeared into the kitchen and returned with two odd-size knives, two plates, one coated with crumbs.

She looked into Tilly's eyes shining with greedy anticipation, handed her the larger knife, her lips forming the first smile they had known since the night Dorothea died, said shyly, "You cut it."

"I'm starving," Tilly admitted, fish and chips no longer even a memory. She cut the cake into two halves, then each into half again, and handed Violet her quarter, before she buried her teeth into her own.

"Shall we sit down? I don't often have company . . . that is the kind of company I find congenial." Violet put the cake down on the plate, and for the first time alluded to Dorothea's death. "You see, my sister died a little while ago and now I have to live by myself."

Tilly leaned forward in her chair. "I found a dead man in the wood opposite. The next day the police came and took my fingerprints. Didn't you read about it in the newspapers?"

She waited for Miss Madden's response. There was none. Violet, plate on her knee, made no attempt to eat the cake. Like a spectre looking over her shoulder, Violet remembered the policeman at the door, politely but firmly inching himself into the house, asking questions she couldn't answer, sitting in Dorothea's chair, catechising and confusing her.

"Didn't you?" Tilly prompted.

Violet shook her head.

"What a shame. Never mind, there'll be the inquest. I telephoned the police. If I hadn't spotted the corpse lying there, it might have been years before anyone found him, and then he'd only have been bones. It was lucky that I went into the wood to look for the weasel." She eyed Miss Madden's plate. "Aren't you going to eat your cake?"

Violet covered her eyes to hide the tears that burst through her lids.

It took Tilly a while to make out the name that was drowned in successive sobs. Sammy. A cat. The death of a human being, like old Mr. Harris who'd lived next door to them at home, and hadn't been outside his house for over a year, the dead man in the woods, never remotely touched the fibres of her pity. But a kitten, a little tabby kitten, run over and killed as it raced towards its mistress! Grief and horror and agonising pity spumed up in her.

She crouched at Miss Madden's feet, one hand holding her dirt-stained fingers, the other gently stroking the tears away.

"No one cared; no one misses him but me."

"I care. I care dreadfully," Tilly swore, and told her about Rufus, the postcards. About the weasel, the squirrel she'd tamed so that he would eat peanuts from her hand but no one else's.

Gradually the comfort of shared sorrow established itself between them, a union of two hearts that poured all their love not on humans but on four-legged dumb animals. Suddenly Tilly bethought herself of the bag of caramels she'd left in the hall, fetched them, counted them out into two equal pyramids —fortunately there was an even number—put one on the table beside Miss Madden's uneaten cake. "They're creamy ones. If you don't chew too hard, they last for ages." She unwrapped one and popped it into Miss Madden's mouth. "Are you sure you don't want to eat your cake?"

"No, dear. Would you like it?"

Tilly ate the cake and Violet, sucking the caramel, tried to remember when last she'd been in the company of a child. So long, so very long ago, that the skinny little form packed into tight clothes seemed to belong to a new species.

Tilly, normally resistant to the passage of time, became conscious that it was a vital factor if she was to visit the wood, bring herself up to date on the developments at the scene of the crime, and looked round for a clock, found one on the mantelshelf. "Your clock's stopped. Did you know? It says five minutes to twelve."

"Yes, it stopped a long time ago. And the alarm clock upstairs. I don't know . . ." Her voice trailed into silence. Dorothea had always wound the clocks, demanded at breakfast, "Did you remember to wind your watch?"

Her lips trembled. "I have a watch, but I can't seem to find it." She looked with anguish at Tilly. "I keep wondering if one of the men who come knocking at my door stole it."

"Maybe they did." Tilly leaned forward, speaking as one with glad tidings to impart. "Mrs. Watts who lives in our road had all her wedding presents stolen while she was on her honeymoon. A canteen of cutlery, the stereo, and all her new clothes. And a mink jacket that had been a wedding present from her husband. She cried for days, but the police never found the burglars."

Receiving no response, she looked at the sad, shrivelled face, the idea dawning, but not accepted, as she fingered the watch she'd transferred to the pocket of her jeans, unprepared to commit herself to an act of such monumental beneficence. If Miss Madden had broken all the clocks, carelessly allowed a watch to be lost or stolen, how could she trust her with a real gold one! Yet, of its own accord her hand took it out of her pocket.

It lay in her palm, glistening, its back delicately engraved with twined but illegible initials, and a date. June 10, 1911. She thought of Rufus waiting for her, of Sammy dead, and she held out her hand. "I can only lend it to you. Just lend. It's not for keeps. And you can't wear it because the strap's broken, but you can put it on the table by you and take it to bed with you at night."

"Oh, I couldn't." Violet looked shocked. "It's real gold, a beautiful gentleman's watch."

"It's only a lend. I'm not giving it to you."

Violet was confused. On the one hand, it would be a comfort to know the time, but its temporary ownership would burden her with another responsibility. "No, dear."

But Tilly wasn't listening. The woods beckoning, she grabbed her share of the caramels. "I'll come and see you again, and you can give me the watch back then."

She went so swiftly that Violet wasn't absolutely sure the child called Tilly wasn't one of the images that slipped in and out of her head, appearing and disappearing, one moment consoling, the next leaving her adrift on a cold tide of desolation.

Then she saw the minute hand on the beautiful watch was moving, stretched her hand towards the caramels, unwrapped one, put it on her tongue. The dark-eyed spidery child was flesh and blood. A little girl who'd shared her tears and promised to come back. She sighed content. Caramels were infinitely more to her taste than Meals on Wheels. Soft and sweet, and there was another word that began with S. Miraculously it came to mind. Sustaining! Proud of herself for remembering it, she fell asleep.

*

Tilly surveyed the wood from her vantage point straddled across the gate. She slid to the ground, walked slowly, holding disappointment at bay. They couldn't have finished already! But the site beneath the bank had been raked, and unless you'd seen the dead man under the coverlet of ivy and brambles there was no evidence that he had ever lain there, that policemen had hidden him inside a tent and carried out a procedure familiar to addicts of television crime series.

She sat on the bank brooding, her sense of justice outraged. She'd found the dead man, but for her he'd have been lying there still. No one had thanked her or praised her for the speed with which she'd summoned the police. And there was no sign of the weasel! Maybe he was dead too, smothered by the man's corpse falling on top of him! A snivel of tears contorted her face. She wiped them away with the back of her hand, decided that when she reached the top of the lane, she'd turn in the opposite direction from Srinagar, walk into the police station. She couldn't believe they didn't want to interview her.

But when Tilly reached the fork, Mrs. Baker was hurrying towards her, as fast as her bunions would permit. She grabbed Tilly's hand so hard that it hurt. "And where have you been, Miss Mischief?" Fear of retribution for the afternoon's nap, made her voice as shrill as a corn-crake's.

"To post my letters."

"That's a downright lie. The pillar-box is fifty yards from the house. Five minutes is all that it would have taken you, and you've been missing for hours. Give your granny a heart attack, you will."

"I went for a walk. I go for walks at home. I'm not a baby. You're hurting my hand."

"What you do at home is your mum's business. What you get up to here is your grandma's, and when she's out, mine. It's not natural, forever haunting the place where a man has been murdered. Regular little ghoul you are. You ought to be ashamed of yourself."

"I'm a witness."

"Rubbish. Messing about with corpses! It isn't healthy. You'll stay in the house till your grandmother gets home. She's got enough to worry her without having to search the woods for you."

"What's she got to worry about?"

"You for a start, and your granddad as he is." She hustled Tilly through the door, gave her a shove towards the kitchen. "Tea's on the table."

Tilly wrinkled her nose with disdain. "I'm not hungry." Cake and caramels made a satisfying diet.

"Suit yourself, but it won't be any good trying to sneak out. The back and front door keys are safe in my pocket, and there they'll stay until your gran gets home."

Tilly lay on the bed, hugging Kipper and sucking caramels, working on an escape route: down the drain-pipe to the tool shed roof, along the ridge, then down another pipe that would bring her within jumping reach of the ground. Before she had finally committed herself to the venture, satiated with sweetness she, like Violet, fell fast asleep.

FIVE

The wives of professional soldiers are trained to keep their emotions under wraps. Nelia's cheeks were dry as she sipped her third gin, but within her was a chaos of creeping despair.

While Reggie was in a cubicle being helped into his clothes by a nurse, she questioned the consultant who had returned to his office where, every nerve prickling with dread, she had waited for an hour. "How is he, doctor?"

A dumpy man, with a cherubic face, pale ginger hair that touched his collar ("Who does he think he is, a pop star?" Reggie jeered. "He can't be a day under fifty!") had given Nelia the professional, meaningless smile he had brought to a fine art. "There is no need to be over-anxious. But his blood pressure is up, quite considerably. So we must watch that."

"I do."

"I'm sure," he murmured. "His heart? Well, again that needs to be constantly monitored but, as I say, no cause for alarm."

"You're saying that his heart and blood pressure have deteriorated since the last time you examined him?"

"Oh, I wouldn't say that."

His refusal to commit himself—when that was what he was being paid handsomely to do—sharpened her tongue. "Then what would you say? When will he be fit enough to undergo the operation on his hip, be released from pain?"

"Mrs. Furston, as I have explained on several occasions, it is a comparatively simple operation. But, alas"—again the false smile surfaced—"before your husband undergoes surgery we need to get him into better shape."

"You're saying his general condition is poor?"

His pursed mouth reprimanded her. "Mrs. Furston, you really must not put words into my mouth. Your husband's blood count is low, his heart is subject to irregularities, and his blood pressure is higher than we would like it to be. Our aim must be to improve and stabilise his general condition. As soon as we have achieved this objective he will be in a condition to undergo surgery." He rang a bell. A film-star nurse entered with four prescription slips which she handed to him before silently withdrawing with a grace that suggested she was floating.

He handed the slips to Nelia. "Inderal, as before, for blood pressure, but a slightly increased dosage. A stronger pain-killer, but on no account is he to take more than three tablets in one day. His usual sleeping pills. I've also prescribed some mild tranquillisers. They should help to relieve the stress, a very important factor. Make an appointment with my receptionist, and I'll see him in three months. Meanwhile, I'll send a full report to your own doctor. Oh, after the exertions of today, I suggest you keep him in bed tomorrow. But up the day after. It is essential he is mobile."

He stood, leaned across the desk to touch the tips of her fingers and, at some pre-arranged signal, the floating girl ushered her out.

Reggie, his face puce, was waiting in the cubicle. "Well, what's the verdict? Out with it."

"That you're doing splendidly. Dr. Meredith is very pleased with you. He's changed some of your pills to milder ones, and he says it won't be long before they operate on your hip."

Instead of cursing, he gave her one of his rare, loving smiles, ruefully shook his head. "Nelia, you're the worst liar in the world. Transparent as a pane of glass. Come on, for God's sake, let's get out of this morgue!"

*

At the sound of the front door-bell, Nelia jerked upright in her chair. Ten-fifteen. She knew of no friend or acquaintance familiar with the routine of the household who would call at this hour. More likely a gang of hooligans playing the age-old trick of ringing a door-bell, then hiding, smothering their mirth at the resulting bafflement of the occupant appearing at the open door. If so, she'd deny them the satisfaction of making a fool of her.

She gulped down the remainder of her drink, stared at herself in a mirror above the fireplace. A wreck! Not a hair straightened, nose powdered since the hired car had delivered them to Srinagar with Reggie to support up the stairs, the children to be fed and bedded down. Thin as a rake, bony, she could have passed for seventy.

When the bell rang a second time, she ignored it, but when it sounded again, the pressure more prolonged, exasperation choked in her throat. The ringing could wake Reggie from his drugged sleep or, worse, Tilly might come leaping down the stairs to announce that someone was at the front door. To avoid either, it seemed she must find out who was bothering her at that time of night—probably someone asking for directions to an address she'd never heard of!

She opened the door about six inches, guarding it with her foot, so that she could slam it instantly.

"Mrs. Furston?"

"Yes."

"I'm Mrs. Rampton. Mrs. Garth Rampton."

The wife or ex-wife of the murdered man! Nelia could conceive of no reason why she should be on her doorstep. Aware that she should have offered some conventional expression of condolence, the words refused to form on her tongue.

Anna advanced a step nearer the door. In the past twenty-four hours time had been suspended. She took no account of whether it was night or day. "It is a matter that concerns your granddaughter. I wish to see her, at once."

For a second stark disbelief at the woman's effrontery held Nelia dumb, then she burst into indignation. "A child, at this hour of the night! She's in bed, asleep. You can't possibly see her."

"I have a right to question the child who found my husband's body. Open the door." When Nelia did not obey, she shouted, "I shall stand here ringing the bell until you do."

Nelia believed her, decided that the only excuse for her extraordinary behaviour was that she was unhinged by grief. She opened the door just wide enough for Mrs. Rampton to squeeze eel-like into the hall. An intimidating woman, with a white, drained look, malevolent eyes: a hating face. Nelia took a grip of herself, spoke in her best *mem-sahib* manner. "Please be good enough to keep your voice down. I have an invalid husband who must on no account be disturbed."

"And a thieving granddaughter!"

Nelia drew in her breath, straightened her shoulders. She had never in her life been involved in a brawl, and had no intention of being challenged to one now. "Purely by chance my granddaughter discovered your husband's body. Then, with admirable presence of mind, she instantly reported it to the police who took the appropriate action."

Anna's mouth curved in derision at the pathetic bean-pole of a woman! She'd spent the last twenty-four hours establishing the identity of the child who'd robbed her husband's corpse, a frustrating exercise, culminating in a blank refusal by the police to name her. Then, she'd run into Sylvia Armitage, a regular customer at Annabel's, a born gossip, and learned that the child was Matilda Allenby, who was staying temporarily with her grandparents at Srinagar along the Ridgeway.

"Before she called the police your granddaughter stole my husband's watch. It was not among his personal effects, and the police swear that when they moved his body to the mortuary he was not wearing a watch. So where is it? I suggest you wake her and find out."

Nelia drew deep on her breath, squared her thin, sloping shoulders, her righteous indignation held under control by a dread of Tilly running downstairs, tripping over her nightgown and falling straight into the arms of a demented woman, screaming, waking Reggie, who would totter to the head of the stairs and maybe fall, lie there helpless. For a moment she ached with yearning for her old bearer in India who would never have permitted her to be bullied by a woman who was clearly out of her mind. With arms outspread to protect her rear she walked backwards to the stairs. "My granddaughter will on no account be disturbed. You will not be allowed to see her. Furthermore, if you don't leave this house immediately I shall telephone Detective Chief Superintendent Deacon who is a close friend of my husband and ask for you to be forcibly removed."

Anna gave a hoot of derision. "Friends in high places! Much good may they do you. My husband's watch was an heirloom. Your granddaughter will produce it in the morning, or she'll be charged with theft."

Nelia's thin bony forefinger pointed at the door. "Leave my house instantly." She was prepared, if she could evict the woman in no other way, to manhandle her.

Anna jibed, "The police! Not, as you appear to believe, paragons of virtue, but more than willing to receive a commendation for restoring stolen property to its rightful owner. The next time you see me, I'll have one in tow." Then, in her black cape that lent her a batlike appearance, she whirled, was gone.

Nelia subsiding on the bottom stair became conscious of whimpers and moans emerging from her throat. If only she could be sure. But, of course, she could be sure. Tilly wasn't a thief, a robber of corpses. Laboriously, as though her bones had aged ten years in as many minutes, she climbed the stairs, pressed her ear to the door panel of their bedroom, listening to Reggie's breathing, his occasional snores, before she began to climb the second flight, where the light burned on the landing.

She eased open Tilly's door. Asleep, her face buried in the pillow, one arm thrown protectively over the moth-eaten donkey, the other hidden under the pillow. Fortunately the furniture was minimal: a chest of drawers, a wardrobe, a table under the window, a smaller one by the bed. Knowing she'd never rest until she'd proved Tilly's innocence, she eased open the drawers, explored their contents with her fingers: underwear, jerseys, a pack of cards, two caramels. She felt in every pocket of the garments hanging in the wardrobe, even fumbled in the toes of the shoes.

Her breath had steadied, she was beginning to relax when her eyes were drawn to the hand thrust under the pillow. Was it curled round a stolen watch? Without warning her knees turned to water and she clung to the bed-rail for support, every shred of moral courage drained out of her. Cravenly she didn't want to know whether Tilly was innocent or guilty.

*

Edmund Lang sat hunched in his car, eyes between their heavy lids fixed on the house. For the sixth time in half an hour, he checked his watch. 11:15 P.M. Where the hell was Anna? Sitting in a pub, drinking herself stupid? Driving recklessly to nowhere? Or, worse still, giving a repeat performance of last night's scene at Fernwell police station, when she'd inveigled a newly-appointed desk sergeant, who'd accepted her credentials as *bona fide*, to view "her husband's" body, examine his effects. A fact he'd only learned this morning when he'd telephoned Deacon to enquire the outcome of the post-mortem, and had been asked to explain his sister's right to claim a relationship that, in law, no longer existed. Edmund had apologised, put in a plea that his sister was suffering from severe shock. Deacon in one of his curt moods informed Edmund the coroner's inquest would be at 10 A.M. on Thursday. He would be required to attend. No question of suicide. Rampton had been murdered.

Shock! He repeated the word as a blanket excuse for Anna's flight from reason: assuming the rôle of Garth's widow, a status that now belonged to Carol. He accepted that the responsibility for coaxing or coercing her back to rational behaviour was his, while inwardly resenting the inroads it made on his concentration, deflecting even momentarily his absorption in every detail of the aftermath of Rampton's death. For weeks, maybe months, he would have to guard every word that passed his lips, monitor each move the police made.

Nerves thrumming, he leapt out of the car, strode up to the

house, fingering the key in his pocket, not certain whether or not Anna was aware it was still in his possession and, if he used it, what in her present state her reaction would be. He took a chance, slid it into the key-hole, left the door open behind him to give warning of his presence, and set about switching on the lights, pouring himself a double Scotch. That swallowed, his long legs ate up the stairs: there was a chance that she'd swallowed a sleeping pill, was lying doped on the bed. The bed was made, the room empty. He switched on the light in the adjacent room, blinked at the shambles of disorder that met his eye: a miscellany of female garments draped over chairs, stools, spilled on the floor. A sort of mammoth jumble sale. He picked up a handful of chiffon, examined it. Not some discarded rag, as he'd supposed, but a hand-sewn garment that had never been worn, the price-tag clipped to the hem. He stooped, gathered up an armful of shoes, inspected the soles. Brand new. A coat, dresses, silk shirts, pants, underwear galore, plus the satin dressing-gown she'd been wearing when he'd broken the news to her of Garth's death. Baffled, unease deepening, he only knew that she'd spent a small fortune on clothes to kit herself out like a bride. And worn none of them since she'd lurched out of the room to be sick in the downstairs cloak-room. But whose bride? A dead man's? He shook his head. Crazy. Anyway, the timing was awry. She'd not known, could not have known, that Garth was dead when she'd indulged in that super spending spree. He ground his teeth in frustration. To be baffled, left without a logical answer constituted for him a small purgatory.

At the sound of a car screeching to a halt, he leapt downstairs, was waiting for her in the lighted porch. Half-way up the path she stumbled, and he was only just in time to keep her from falling. Relief was instant: Anna was drunk. He put his arm round her shoulder. "Easy does it."

She snatched herself out of his grasp, walked without one uncertain step into the house, shed her cloak. "Pour me a drink. I've news for you." She sat down, hands braced on her splayed knees, eyes crowing with glee. When she'd swallowed the drink, she waved her glass aloft. "Congratulate me! I've run to earth the child delinquent who stole Garth's watch."

He was conscious of a barely perceptible pause between one heart-beat and the next. "What watch?"

Her glance flayed him with contempt. "His father's watch. The one he always wore and which the police swore blind they'd never seen."

He summoned its image to his eye. Had it been on Garth's wrist when he'd dragged the near-corpse into the parking yard? His normally acute memory failed him. He simply did not know. "So you got it back?"

"That's your job. When I went to collect it, the old harridan of a grandmother refused to let me see the child. Barred the stairs. The precious little innocent was asleep, not to be disturbed." She refilled her glass. "A withered old hag who behaved like a grand duchess, threatened to call the police. Not that it would have done her any good. That child stole Garth's watch." She jabbed the air with a grimy finger. "So, first thing in the morning you will drive to the house on the Ridgeway and reclaim it. It's mine."

To divert her attention from an order he had no intention of fulfilling, he said, "The inquest is at ten o'clock."

"Then immediately it is over. It's stolen property. My property."

For a moment he considered facing her with the brutal truth: that, in law, she had no claim to Garth's possessions. The venom on her face, in her voice, warned him that he would be wasting his breath. He side-tracked. "Anna, I suggest you don't attend the inquest. Spare yourself that ordeal. At this stage, it's no more than a formality: murder by person or persons unknown."

"Unknown!" She rolled the word on her tongue, then laughed. "The police may not choose to know!" Almost flippantly she shrugged her shoulders. "Anyway, I'm going."

He moistened his under-lip. "Carol will be there."

She lifted her glass, drained it, wilfully deaf to his caution.

He said with genuine pity, "Anna, don't make it harder for yourself than you need."

Her eyes were hooded, making a barrier between them. When she spoke she emphasised each syllable. "My husband was brutally murdered. I have a right to attend the inquest. At least I'll hear and remember all the filthy lies."

His ear caught, or imagined it caught, a nuance of insinuation. He rejected it, and met full on her sunken, brooding eyes examining every millimetre of his face. His discomfiture was slight, no more than as if someone had drawn a finger-nail across his flesh. Anna, he told himself, was easing her grief—if grief it was—by needling him with accusations which could have no basis in fact. She didn't possess second-sight! No more than an intuitiveness sharper than the norm, but that didn't invest her with the power to telescope the forty miles that had divided them on the night when the heart of the near-corpse had ceased to function.

He stood up, forced himself to place a comforting hand on her shoulder. "If there's anything I can do, you've only to ask."

"There isn't unless you can tell me who blew Garth's brains out." She lifted her head, eyes black slits. "Can you?"

"For God's sake!"

She repeated after him: "Yes, indeed, for God's sake!"

He moved back a couple of steps. "Try to get some sleep. Take a pill if you have to. I'll pick you up at ten."

"Don't bother. I'm perfectly capable of driving myself."

At the door he paused, looking at her looking at him, made one final plea. "At an inquest everyone is on show. It's like a theatre stage. Anna, try and pull yourself together."

She nodded twice. "I've never been more pulled together as you put it in my whole life." That was the truth. In the storm of anguish there was an eye of quietude in that Garth was hers forever, to the rim of her life and beyond.

She called after him, "Don't forget to reclaim Garth's watch, from Matilda Allenby, granddaughter of a retired colonel. Furston's the name. Put the fear of God into the brat, and if that fails, have the police issue a search warrant."

When he turned, her head was lowered, anger spent, smiling to herself. What he had no means of knowing was that, the instant the door closed, Garth's voice would sound in her ear.

＊

At two o'clock in the morning, Nelia arrived at a possible solution. At eight, apologising for the early call, she telephoned Anthea Grant, whose father had been a subaltern in her husband's regiment, and was now a business executive, who lived two miles outside Anderbridge.

Abjectly begging a favour, backtracking, repeating herself, it took Anthea a while to unravel the favour Nelia was begging. "You want me to have the two children for the day? Is that it?"

"I hate to be a nuisance, and I'm sure it's terribly inconvenient at such short notice, but I would be terribly grateful. Oh, darling, could you?"

"Of course. Nothing simpler," which was far from the truth. Anthea's husband had dropped the car at the station garage for servicing, was due to pick it up this evening. No transport. Jeremy, her elder son, was camping in Wales, which left Nicholas, the less co-operative of the two, who was currently working through what his parents called one of his "broody spells." He'd surface in his own good time, but meanwhile he never uttered two words if one would suffice. And, since she was half-way through painting Jeremy's bedroom, she'd planned a scratch soup and salad lunch.

Nelia's voice quavered on, jumping gnatlike from one subject to another: Uncle Reggie's health, a crazy woman who was some unspecified threat to Tilly and something about a watch that Tilly hadn't stolen, while Anthea sifted through a list of friends who'd lend her a car. Then suddenly the substance of Nelia's outpourings percolated through to her and she gave a gasp of horror. "You mean that it was Tilly who actually found Garth Rampton in the wood! What a hideous experience for a child. Of course, I understand. She must be terribly shaken."

Nelia's voice quavered. "It's not that so much. It's hard to explain. She almost seems proud of herself."

Anthea laughed comfortingly. "All children are ghouls. A bird drops dead here we're treated to a full-dress burial service." She explained about the transport. "It'll probably be Marcia Wain who'll pick them up. Spectacular blonde, with gorgeous long legs. Say around ten-thirty. That okay?"

"Yes, dear, and I'm oh so grateful."

When Nelia turned away from the telephone she faced a sullen-faced Tilly in the doorway.

"Are we going somewhere?"

"Yes, indeed you are." Nelia put on what was intended to be a smile of congratulation at the rare treat ahead. "Mrs. Grant, whom I've known since she was not much older than you, and now has two little boys of her own has invited you and Miles to spend the day with them. They've a lovely garden with a swing and a slide, and there's a swimming pool. Oh, you're going to have a wonderful time."

"Boys!"

"Yes, boys. One just about your age."

"I can't go."

"Whyever not? I've accepted Mrs. Grant's kind invitation. Of course you're going."

"The inquest is this morning. I'm a witness. They'll want to question me."

"What nonsense! Little girls are not allowed to attend inquests." Curiosity got the better of her. "How did you know it was being held today?"

"I asked the boy who delivered the newspapers. He knew all about it."

"Nonsense," Nelia repeated. "Your grandfather would never allow it. And neither would your parents. It is quite out of the question, so no more arguments. Come along, breakfast is ready."

"But I'm a witness," Tilly wailed. "I found the body. I found it first."

"No one under twelve is eligible to be a witness." If that was not true, it ought to be. "They have to produce a birth certificate. So you will please come and eat your breakfast, make your bed, tidy yourself and be ready to leave for the Grants at ten-thirty."

The adamancy in her grandmother's voice temporarily silenced Tilly. Then hope spurted. "Have they got a dog?"

"Yes," Nelia said, praying she was speaking the truth.

"What kind?"

Nelia, reduced to a state of quiet desperation, closed her eyes. "I don't know. Do you think you could stop asking questions I can't answer? Your grandfather is spending the day in bed, which means I'll be running up and down stairs all the morning."

"I wonder why Grandfather doesn't have a dog. It would keep him company, and he could train it to retrieve all the things he drops and can't pick up."

Nelia's gaze by-passed Tilly, concentrated on dear Miles standing at the cooker, spooning fat over a frying egg. "Oh, how kind of you, Miles dear. But don't fry an egg for me, toast will be sufficient."

Tilly crowed, "He knows you never eat fried eggs, that's why he's cooked four, so that he can have two."

*

Immediately the coroner had pronounced his verdict, Anna stalked out of court, like a tragedy queen, Edmund thought as he followed her. The shabby black cloak slung over a dark dress. He supposed he should be thankful she wasn't wearing a widow's veil.

He opened the door of her car. Without so much as a glance in his direction she got in, sat behind the steering wheel, seemingly playing a new rôle: dignified remoteness, total withdrawal into herself. She made no comment on the evidence, on the police statements, including a written one taken from the child. She'd not, as he'd dreaded, stood up in court, harangued the coroner. In fact, she'd behaved impeccably.

He bent his head to the open window. "I'll look in, shall I, around eight this evening?"

"If you like."

He watched her drive through the archway into Fernwell High Street. She hadn't reminded him to reclaim the watch, as though a drama that had obsessed her the previous night had been obliterated by another, more important. There had been none of those sly, incisive glances that threatened to make dents in the protective armour in which he clad himself. In its place, a deliberate snapping of the bond that had always existed between them. In grief or disaster they'd always drawn close together. But not now. It was as if, somehow, she knew something which she could not possibly know.

The clothes, luxury goods, with couturier labels stitched into them, were an itch at the back of his mind. A conundrum he couldn't solve. Granted that women were notoriously subject to buying sprees, but not Anna. Though clothes were her trade she rarely spent lavishly on herself. Too high-fashion, too expensive for the boutique, she could only have bought them for herself. And not, to his knowledge worn one, only garbed herself in the shabbiest clothes she possessed.

The edge of his vision was distracted by Carol Rampton, enveloped in a tartan shawl, being helped into a car by her father. He was about to walk over and offer her his sympathy when he felt the heavy clamp of a hand on his shoulder.

"Sorry if I startled you, but I wondered if we could have a word? In your office. A radiator at headquarters has sprung a leak. Plumbers everywhere. Not to mention a clutch of supermen detectives straight out of college. All bright-eyed and bushy-tailed, hell bent on instant fame and promotion."

Edmund glanced sideways at the burly, late middle-aged form, the jowled face cunningly shaped into benignity that was a form of deceit. Deliberately he ignored Deacon's forward pace. "I don't see the point. Apart from the evidence I submitted to the coroner, I made a full statement to your inspector. He interviewed each member of the staff, went over the office with a fine tooth comb, and presumably followed the same procedure at the Fernwell head office and our Camfort branch. There really is nothing I can add."

"I know." Superintendent Deacon flapped a hand in vague agreement. "But it's remarkable how minor facts, seemingly irrelevant, sometimes jell when you go over the ground a second time. If we toss the ball around for half an hour we may turn up something. And, heaven knows, we need it. From the reports that lie on my desk you'd think Garth Rampton hadn't an enemy in the world. Yet every man has one, somewhere. Most times he's a sleeper, biding his time."

"Drive to Anderbridge and back to Fernwell? Isn't that a waste of your time?"

"Time wasted is a hazard that goes with the job. Counterbalanced by a chauffeur-driven police car. Since you'll need your own, you can follow on behind."

The Anderbridge office occupied a corner site in the town, its two plate-glass windows furnished with blown-up photographs of properties on the market, the centre-piece a baronial castle. In passing, Deacon gave it a nod. "Make a cosy country seat for an Arab sheik!"

Edmund's smile was minimal. He led him through the handsomely designed ground floor offices, past a projection room from which a faint whirring was audible.

"Ah, yes! I'd heard you'd gone into the film business. Clients approve?"

"Yes. Relieves them of the tedium of driving to half a dozen sites. Now they sit in comfort and make a preliminary choice."

"Art deceiving the eye?"

A cliché Edmund did not consider worthy of comment. He motioned Deacon to the chair in which the near-corpse had sat.

"Bit low for me," Deacon murmured and transferred himself to a fake Chippendale arm-chair. "I knew old Rampton, you know, though he was getting on by then. Shrewd, never wasted a penny, but never cheated you, either."

"Superintendent . . ."

"Yes, yes. I appreciate you're pushed for time, and I don't intend to trespass on much of it. How long have you been manager here?"

"Just coming up to three years."

"Would it be fair to say that, with the boss as a brother-in-law, you enjoyed a privileged position?"

"I'd question that. I earned my promotion. Also, Garth Rampton was the last man who could be accused of nepotism."

"Agreed. After your sister divorced him you remained on good terms?"

"Yes."

"How often were you in touch?"

"By telephone most days. On an average he looked in here two or three times a week."

"The last occasion being on the evening of the night he was murdered?"

"Yes."

"Give me a run-down on what happened. Oh, yes, I know you made a full statement to Detective Inspector Warren, which is on file, but it might throw up some minor detail, a chance remark that could provide us with a clue as to where Rampton went after he left here." He settled his well-padded muscular form a little more comfortably in the chair, folded his hamlike fists in his lap. "Let me recap. He dropped in around six o'clock, after the office had closed at five-thirty. Three of the staff were still on the premises: you, your secretary, Audrey Pembury, and a junior, Roy Allsop. Rampton exchanged a few words with Miss Pembury and Allsop, then walked into your office. Were you expecting him? Had he telephoned ahead?"

"No, but I wasn't unduly surprised to see him. He often looked in about that time if he wanted to discuss a particular property. In this case it was the Malden Hill estate which is due to be auctioned in a month's time. We discussed the lots into which it should be divided."

"For how long?"

"Until approximately half-past seven."

"By which time he'd made his decision?"

"Not finally. He said he'd sleep on it, and asked me to telephone him next morning." Edmund flipped over his desk calendar. "At ten-thirty. I did so, and his secretary told me he hadn't yet arrived at the office."

"What time did Miss Pembury and young Allsop leave?"

"Approximately six-fifteen. Miss Pembury handed me the keys."

"And that was the only subject you discussed: the Malden Hill sale? For an hour and a quarter!"

"Yes. It was a complex sale. It could have been split up in a variety of ways."

"And then, at seven-thirty P.M.?"

"I saw him to his car in the parking yard, came back here, put some papers in the safe, locked up and drove home."

"With his wife away, did he give you any hint as to where he was going to spend the rest of the evening?"

"No. I assumed he would drive straight home. But I could have been wrong."

"His car was found abandoned in a lay-by off the Cotteshall Road, which was certainly not on his route home. Keys, wiped clean, in the ignition. No fingerprints. Forensic vacuumed it. Usual dust, fluff, but nothing to give us a firm lead. What happened after you'd seen Rampton off the premises?"

"I checked the locks, then picked up my own car from the yard, drove home."

Deacon mused. "To Lane End. Bit isolated for an up-and-coming man like you, surely?"

Edmund gestured towards the windows. "Even with double-glazing I spend eight to nine hours a day deafened by cars, lorries, juggernauts, stopping and starting up at the traffic lights. Peace and quiet can be a luxury."

Deacon sighed ill-humouredly. "I doubt if I'll live to see the ring road they've been arguing over for twenty years. And you drove straight home?"

"Straight home. Estimated time of arrival eight o'clock."

"Out again?"

"Only into the garden. I sprayed some rose bushes to kill the greenfly."

"With his wife away, no meal waiting for him, any idea where Rampton might be likely to eat his evening meal?"

"None. Maybe a pub."

"We've checked them all. None of his neighbours saw him drive in. Quarter of a mile away are a couple, the Cruickshaws, who were giving a drinks party to which Rampton had been invited. He would have passed their house on his way home. He never turned up. Neither did he telephone, make his excuses. Yet he was a courteous man, wouldn't you have said? Not the type to stand his hostess up?"

"I would."

"So it would seem that on that particular evening he acted out of character?"

"Yes."

There was an arid pause during which Edmund re-aligned the files on his desk. When he looked up it was to meet head-on Deacon's eyes between their puffy lids. "With the exception of the murderer, you would appear to be the last person to have seen the deceased alive."

"Not necessarily. There's a wide time gap. My last sight of Garth was around seven-thirty P.M. when I saw him into his car. I understand from your inspector that the estimated time of death was approximately two A.M. A lapse of seven hours! I hope you're lucky and run to earth someone who saw him after he left here."

"I'll second that."

Deacon leaned forward to ease his bulk out of the chair. "Well, I won't take up any more of your time." As Edmund opened the door, Deacon put out his hand and closed it. "About your sister, Mr. Lang. I appreciate that she's emotionally disturbed and I make allowances for the shock she's suffered, but I'd be grateful if you could persuade her to behave a little more, well, shall we say, discreetly. Last night, at a late hour, she distressed Mrs. Furston, the wife of Colonel Furston who lives on the Ridgeway, by accusing her seven-year-old granddaughter, the child who found Rampton, of stealing his watch. Colonel Furston, a cripple, with a dicky heart, altogether not in too good shape, telephoned me this morning, said he was not prepared to have his wife abused and intimidated in her own house."

"I'm sorry. At the moment my sister isn't entirely rational. I'll have a word with her. But I suppose it is possible that the child could have picked up the watch?"

"Her grandfather has questioned her. Her room, clothes, every possible hiding-place have been searched. She swears she hasn't got the watch. Colonel Furston dealt with her pretty sternly, I understand, so I think we can assume she wouldn't dare lie to him."

"Perhaps I should telephone Mrs. Furston, apologise, explain the circumstances?"

"Leave well alone. The child has been sent to stay with friends. Just make sure there is no repetition of last night's scene." Reaching for the door, he took a pace backwards, bringing the two of them abruptly against one another, only inches dividing them. "A bit odd we can't trace it, the watch I mean. Mrs. Rampton says that when he drove her to her parents' home she thought he was wearing it, but she can't swear to it. Was it on Rampton's wrist the evening he called here?"

"I don't remember noticing it. But sitting facing a wall clock there was no reason for him to glance at it."

Deacon brooded. "We're checking the local jewellers but so far we've drawn a blank. If he'd sent it farther afield for repairs his secretary would have seen to the packing, which she was not asked to do. Valuable, it seems, belonged to his grandfather, engraved with his initials. What amounted to an heirloom. You can't throw any light on it?"

"Sorry."

Deacon held out his hand. "Thanks for your time. I can find my own way out. Hope I haven't made you late for lunch. And don't forget that word in your sister's ear. Peppery type, you know, ex-Indian Army colonels. Well briefed on their rights as citizens."

Edmund stood beside his desk, assessing the interview with Deacon, weighing any potential threat. Deacon was renowned for his faked geniality, for his skill in softening up his victim before he delivered the stiletto thrust, moved in for the kill. He'd not issued a request to call Anna to heel, but an order. But what effect would any ultimatum have on her? A hooting laugh of derision? A blank-eyed glance over the top of a gin and tonic? That unnerving remoteness, a retreat into a private stronghold which he could not penetrate? Impatiently he tossed conjectures to the wind. They got him nowhere.

He lifted the telephone, dialled the number of the boutique. "What do you mean, gone away? How long for?"

"Deacon didn't say."

"Didn't you ask for her address?"

"I doubt if he had it."

"Then he damned well should have it. I don't care if she's in Timbuctoo, I want Garth's watch, even if I have to wring her neck to get it." She slammed down the receiver.

He concentrated hard on the enigma of the watch. He had taken its presence on Garth's wrist for granted, but had no recollection of having actually noticed it. No proof either that it hadn't been there. If he'd been wearing it, the watch would have been on Garth's left wrist. He'd taken the pulse on the right. When the body lurched forward and he'd pulled it upright, had his finger-tips come in contact with the watch-glass, left a tell-tale fingerprint?

He heard a muted sound form on his lips, recognised it as a whimper and, despising himself, stifled it. The alligator strap, rubbed, maybe weakening, could have snapped, been buried in the leaf-mould. But wouldn't the police have sieved every particle?

He gazed about him. Could it have detached itself as he'd hauled Garth across the room, down the corridor and out into the car-park? The possibility of its being found in any part of the office was nil: the cleaner, ultra conscientious, left little piles of pins, paperclips, she had retrieved from the floor on the nearest desk. Then the car-park?

Audrey, hatted, gloved, appeared at the door. "I'm off to lunch, Mr. Lang. You not having any?"

"Just going." He went through the motions of tidying up his desk.

"Right." She closed the door in her usual emphatic manner.

That meant that only young Allsop, the most junior trainee, would be on guard to cover the telephone, munch the sandwiches his mother cut for him, gulp down his can of Coca-Cola. He tried to thrust the watch out of his mind, failed.

He found himself under an irresistible compulsion to examine every inch of the wash-room, the offices and passages, combing the floor-space, thrusting his hands down the sides of the chair in which Garth had sprawled. He even looked inside the drinks cabinet. Eyes still slanted downwards, he walked to the car-park to scotch the one chance in a million that the watch had somehow attached itself to his person, fallen into the yard. Not a sight of it, which must mean that either Garth himself had sent the watch to a London jeweller for repair, or the child who'd found Garth's body had stolen it. In either event there would, by now, be no trace of his fingerprints.

His calm restored, he strode across the road, along the High Street making his way to the outer edge of the town to the Bell and Candle for a snack lunch. He chose a seat at the far end of the bar where the light was dim, hunched his shoulders to screen himself from acquaintances whose only subject of conversation would be the Rampton murder. Luck was with him in that no one approached him, and the only two men with whom he had a nodding acquaintance were too engrossed in their conversation to notice him. Half an hour later he walked out of the dimness of the bar into the clean sunlight.

As he retraced his steps towards the office, he saw coming towards him an old woman, with an uneven gait, her head crowned by a pinkish-red child's bonnet from which hanks of straggling grey hair escaped to dangle about her ears. Automatically his lids snapped shut to deny the evidence of his eyes. When he opened them he was face to face with the old hag he'd seen illuminated in the upward glare of the torch that she'd swung wildly to and fro to spot-light his face as she'd stumbled towards the car, screaming obscenities.

He wheeled, faced the window of a furniture store, waited for her reflection to imprint itself on the glass. When an interminable minute passed without a glimpse of it, he slewed round. She was stationary, forming a blockage on the pavement that people were obliged to circle round, holding some small object against her ear. Listening intently for a reassuring tick before she thrust the watch on its broken strap deep into the pocket of her raggy coat, before, with a hobbling gait she passed him without a glance, intent only on driving her legs to the maximum speed of which they were capable.

When she was a hundred yards ahead of him, he followed, keeping a distance between them. Once clear of Fernwell the houses thinned out, and after thirty minutes' walking he couldn't imagine where she was making for until, as the road straightened, he saw her open the gate of a small isolated cottage behind a hedge midway between Fernwell and Anderbridge that had made no imprint on him when he'd passed it in the car.

The cottage, practically on the roadside, was no more than a couple of hundred yards from the gate into Bateman's Wood. His mind began to race, to print picture after picture in his head, any one of which chilled to ice the blood that flowed through his veins. A night-roamer, had she wandered into the wood, spied on him as he'd dragged the near-corpse to its grave? In the ensuing silence had she heard the shattering explosion of the gun that had half-deafened him? Seen his face in the bright moonlight, recognised it, watched him effacing his footprints in the leaf-mould? Was there some moment lurking in the future when she'd screech to all the world that she'd witnessed him committing murder?

SIX

"I hear you went visiting yesterday," Mrs. Baker remarked. "Have yourselves a good time?"

Tilly grimaced. "It was boring. Granny said they had a dog, but they hadn't. They've never had a dog."

"No pleasing some folks! How about you, young man?"

"It was okay. Nicholas and I swam in their pool." Nicholas, once his mother was out of sight, had seemed intent on drowning Miles by grabbing his legs, holding him under. Miles had been scared stiff; worse, terrified that his panic would be shamefully exposed. "The food was okay."

"It wasn't." Tilly glared at him. "Just bits of lettuce, all soggy, and stringy ham."

Nelia came downstairs with a lighter heart. Dear Reggie, in an emergency, was a tower of strength. "No need to say how long the children are away. It's none of Deacon's business. I've warned him that if that woman attempts to force herself into the house again, I shall demand she's arrested."

"Miles, dear, I wonder if you'd go to the shops for me? To tempt your grandfather's appetite I've decided to make a raspberry mousse for lunch. Two punnets. Buy them at Strawson's where they come straight from their nursery."

Hope leaping, Tilly offered, "I could go."

"Ah, but when would you be back? You're apt to go wandering off goodness knows where, aren't you? And the mousse has to be chilled."

Tilly scowled. "At home I go anywhere I want. No one ever asks me where I've been. Anyway, I'd be with Miles."

Nelia dithered, aware she was falling a victim to weakness.

On the other hand it was becoming impracticable if not impossible to keep Tilly penned in the garden. "If you'll promise you'll stay together. The traffic is heavy at this time in the morning. So mind how you cross the road. Miles, you will be careful, won't you?"

Miles promised. Tilly walked behind, matching her steps to her brother's, who ignored her. In Miles's experience there was only one way to cope with trouble, pretend it didn't exist. And trouble was what his sister would spell before the morning was over. Trouble for which he'd be blamed!

"That's Strawson's," she yelled in his ear, pointing across the road. "You've walked past it."

"You don't bolt across the road anywhere. You use the pedestrian crossing and walk back."

Behind him, Tilly stuck out her tongue, itching to make her escape, confirm with her eyes and ears that the watch was still ticking, that Miss Madden hadn't trodden on it and smashed the glass. As the assistant began to count the change into Miles's hand, she spun about, and when Miles turned, she had vanished.

Humiliated at being tricked by a girl two and a half years his junior, he sprinted along the pavement, peered into shops, crossed the road, looked down side-streets, conscientiously pursuing an exercise he knew was doomed to failure. She'd take jolly good care he didn't see her, even if she was only a few yards away. No alternative presented itself but to plod home and confess.

Nelia, repossessed not only by visions of skidding lorries, sleazy men in dirty rain-coats, but of a physical attack by a demented woman, put a hand to her mouth in horror.

Mrs. Baker made an effort to relieve the gloom. "She's a natural roamer, that one. My Gavin was the same at her age. Many a night he's had his father traipsing the streets for him, but he'd always turn up when he was hungry, and never a scratch on him. Short of tying them up with a dog chain, there's nothing to be done but grin and bear it. Sort of fever they catch. Off to see the rainbow!"

"But girls!" Nelia quavered. "Little girls."

"Tougher than boys these days. Maybe you'd keep her at home more if you had a telly. Kids will sit glued to it all day, good as gold. I've never understood why you don't buy one."

"My husband doesn't care for television. He prefers his radio." A soporific for the masses, reducing them to chair-bound zombies was how Reggie put it. Self-hypnosis. Nelia's sole access to one was by courtesy of Miss Brent who lived alone two doors away, and kept her television switched on from 10:00 A.M. till midnight. For company, she explained, and invited Nelia to pop in whenever she liked. Which Nelia did on the rare occasions when she could make an excuse to leave Reggie, and sat entranced for half an hour. Once she'd been lucky and seen the dear Queen in full colour.

Tilly, who couldn't find a bell on Miss Madden's front door, hammered on it with her knuckles and when that brought no response, raced round to the back. That door was locked too, but at the bottom of the garden a man cutting the hedge held his shears suspended in the air to glower at her.

She galloped down the path, arms flailing. "The doors are locked, and I can't make her hear. Has she gone out?"

Bert Pritchard, who "did" Miss Madden's garden when he felt so inclined, was a man of such skeletal dimensions that he might have been judged to be in his seventies, though in fact that week he'd celebrated his fifty-fifth birthday with a half bottle of Scotch he'd shared with no one. Hair that had been grey for twenty years sprouted in tufts from his pink skull, and the waxy pallor of his skin suggested a delicate constitution. Appearances were deceptive. He could outwork and outstay any man of his age, though he did not choose to earn more money than that required to support his life-style, which he'd reduced to a miracle of simplicity. His voice and manner were truculent. "What do you want?"

"To see Miss Madden." Tilly did a jig of impatience. "It's terribly important."

Cautious to his bones, Bert sniffed. "Never seen you around before. Stranger in these parts, aren't you?"

"No, I'm not. I'm staying with my grandparents, and they've lived here for ages." Anxiety mounting, Tilly pleaded: "It's urgent. I've got to see Miss Madden. Where is she?"

"Locked up." The shears went rhythmically to work. "You'd best leave her alone. She wants a bit of peace and quiet, she does."

Tilly's attention was suddenly diverted by a black and white dog loping towards them with a limp rabbit dangling from its jaws. Quivering with pride it laid the dead offering at its master's feet, wagged its tail to and fro in the undergrowth. Bert Pritchard fondled the dog's head. "There's my girl!"

Tilly burst into tears, clapped the palms of her hands over her eyes. "It's dead," she wailed.

Pritchard's mouth sagged open. "Wouldn't be no good for the pot if it wasn't, now would it?" With uncommon tact he removed the body from sight. "Guess you live in a town, don't you?"

Tilly nodded, snivelled.

"Don't take on so. Nell knows her stuff. Snaps a neck in a trice. That rabbit never felt a thing."

Tilly dropped her hands, looked at the dog. Mr. Pritchard gestured. Nell advanced, licked Tilly's hand. Tears spurted from her eyes. "I do wish animals didn't have to die."

"God's law. Applies to every mortal thing that's alive, us included. All you get is a choice between a hole in the ground and an oven."

"Oh, I don't mind *people* dying." Her eyes bright, tearless, she boasted, "I found the dead man in the wood, the one who was murdered."

"Did you now!"

"You don't believe me, do you. No one does. But I did find him in the wood when I went to see the weasel."

"And did you see the weasel?"

"No."

"Thought as much. Cunning little devils, weasels. Mind you never pick one up, it'd nip off the end of your finger, eat it for supper. Not that you're likely to get the chance."

She looked back at the house. "I must see Miss Madden. I lent her a watch because she'd lost hers and all her clocks had stopped, and I want to make sure she hasn't broken it. It's a very special watch."

Mr. Pritchard ruminated for a full minute before he made his decision. "I'm not letting you in, not without her say-so. She's been plagued enough by a lot of nosy women. But, tell you what, I'll see if I can persuade her to come to a window. Then she can decide for herself whether she wants to see you." The pink-lidded eyes admonished her. "It's up to her. I'm not having her bothered, not after the state she was in when I got here. Been crying her eyes out, she had, was all of a shake. So if she doesn't want to see you, it's no use your pestering. You'd best get off home."

"But I won't pester her, I promise. I never do. We're friends."

Violet, summoned from her bed by Bert's three-tone whistle, clawed her way to the window, rubbed the dust from the centre pane, and there was the little pixie girl.

Tilly squatted cross-legged on the floor by Miss Madden, the watch in the palm of her hand. Miss Madden, wearing the clothes in which she'd slept, heaved a couple of gasping sighs. "There, I feel easier now," and held out her hands, nails rimmed with grime, to the fire Mr. Pritchard had lit. Though she hadn't noticed it, he'd also scooped onto a tray a miscellaneous assortment of dirty crockery and shot it into the sink. Living in a caravan he believed in washing up as he went along.

Tilly, though overjoyed to be re-possessed of the watch, found it difficult to make sense out of the drama that emerged in fits and starts from Miss Madden's lips. There were so many contradictions, half-finished sentences.

"But why did you think someone wanted to steal the watch? Did you hear a burglar? If you did we could telephone the police and ask them to keep a look out so that they can arrest him."

"A burglar?" Violet was confused, constantly distracted by the flickering scenes that skipped through her head and then blacked out, so that she could never recapture what she wanted to remember. Her upper lip shook. "Maybe it was a dream."

"A dream!" Denied the drama, Tilly scolded, "But you said he opened the door, walked in and tried to take the watch from you. That's what you just said."

Violet nodded without conviction.

"Well, then, he was a thief. He ought to be put in prison." Tilly shot to her feet. "He might come back, break in through a window even if all the doors are locked."

Violet bent her head. He might, either in the flesh or as a figure in a nightmare. As sometimes happened, she was granted an interlude of lucidity in which she was aware there were portions of time in which she was incapable of distinguishing between the two. The truth arrived at, she felt strangely at peace. She closed her knotted hand round one of the child's that was small and bony like a bird's claw. "Now I've found my own watch, and have given you back the one you lent me, I shan't worry. It's such a handsome watch you must take care of it."

"Where did you find it, your own watch, I mean?"

Violet couldn't remember, but she said upstairs.

Tilly made one last plea. "But the lights. You talked about them, and a man in a car. You said you'd chased him. You didn't dream that, did you?"

The gauze curtain descended, and all Violet could see, enveloped in the dark shadows of grief, was Sammy's fragile bones shattered, his tiny face bloodied. She bowed her head in her hands and sobbed.

Bert Pritchard walked through the door, took a firm grip of Tilly's shoulder. "Now then, you've been here long enough, and got what you came for, so it's time you took yourself off." Forcibly he turned her to face the door. "I'll make her a strong cup of tea, with plenty of sugar and that'll do her a power of good."

"But she said a burglar tried to steal the watch . . ."

"Off with you. When she has one of her poorly days she doesn't want badgering with a lot of questions." He propelled

Tilly through the front door, and in case she should be tempted to dodge back, locked it behind her.

*

Anna, having parked her car half-way up the lane, sat upright on the bank, a few feet from the coverlet of ivy and bramble that had been transformed into a holy shrine. The gash of red lips in her chalk-white face was made soft, tremulous as she listened to the words of love and loving flowing between them.

Last night he had breathed the name. It had been sealed in her head when she woke, Baby-face Carol, trailing grubby shawls and tatty Hindoo scarves, with a lover who was the father of the child-to-be, plotting to get their thieving paws on Garth's money. She actually saw her hands closing round the stalklike throat, squeezing, squeezing . . .

A twig cracking jerked her eyelids wide apart. Creeping towards her, head bent, was a child: *the* Child! The police had lied. Not hidden away, but scouring the ground for further treasure, Garth's cuff-links maybe, or money that had fallen out of his pocket. Without a whisper of sound Anna rose to her feet, pointed a vermilion tipped finger at Tilly. "Hand it over. The watch you stole from my husband."

Tilly, who'd been looking for the weasel, was struck rigid with shock at the apparition of a witch in a flowing black cloak who had seemingly risen out of the ground like an illustration in one of *Grimm's Fairy Tales* she'd long outgrown. She whirled about, started to run to the gate she'd left open. She was within touching distance of the post when the claw-hands grabbed hold of her, shook her and spat in her face. "You stole my husband's watch. Robbed the dead. Give it to me, you little fiend or I'll hand you over to the police."

Sheer animal terror transformed Tilly into a whirling dervish, kicking, biting, lifting her foot and plunging it hard into Anna's stomach. Released for a second, she bounded through the gate as Anna, winded, rocked on her heels, shouting, "I didn't. I didn't. You're a wicked old witch who tells lies."

And with her lungs hardly capable of drawing breath she ran

until she spied a gap in the hedge, fought her way through it.

Against her thigh she could feel the solid shape of the watch, that was hers because it belonged to no one, except maybe a dead man who wouldn't be able to wear it. She hadn't even lied about it because when Grandfather had made her swear she hadn't stolen it, she'd lent it to Miss Madden—minor prevarications never bothered Tilly. Anyway, the watch was spoken for, destined to be a super, super present for her father.

Farther up the lane she heard a car start up, and hurled herself into a nearby ditch, pulled leaves and dead twigs over her until she'd made herself invisible, a part of the earth itself. She knew it was the witch, driving at a crawl, searching the hedges, and until the car had passed her, and the sound of the engine began to fade, she lay like a wild animal feigning death. She lifted her head, clawed away some of the debris, tears triggered off by shock rather than fright pouring down her cheeks. She smudged them away with the back of her hand. After all, she'd won, beaten the witch, and the watch was still in her pocket. For comfort she eased it out. The filigree hands pointed to ten minutes to twelve. She held it to her ear and listened to the music of the soft tick-tick. She turned it over, stroked the intricate tracery of the initials that she couldn't separate one from the other, wrapped it in a filthy handkerchief and gently tucked it back into her pocket, to keep it safe for her father.

Crawling through the hedge to reach the lane, she tripped, sprawled full-length into a water-logged drain. She wiped the mud off her face, plunged her hands through some rank grass to clean them, and began to trudge up the lane. She pretended to herself that she was with her father, that he'd slid his arms across her shoulder, drawn her close to him, loving the watch, loving her, saying how clever she was to find it.

And he would have done, except that he was hundreds of thousands of miles away.

*

Miles was dispatched by his grandmother to run Tilly to earth, produce her in time for lunch. Deciding it was hopeless to search the town, he placed himself strategically at the junction of the High Street and the lane that skirted Bateman's Wood. That way he could keep watch in three different directions.

At the end of half an hour, when his eyes were beginning to glaze, he saw in the distance a spiderlike creature hauling itself up the steep incline of the lane: a Tilly who had shrunk in size, been robbed of her spritelike agility. In mounting horror he watched her snail-like advance, head bowed, clothes filthy and torn, the single bright note of colour, blood running down her arm.

Fear exploded in his head, froze his wits, glued his feet to the ground, as six months telescoped, pitched him backwards to the day when Samantha, the ten-year-old daughter of the house-matron, came screaming through the school gates, blood running from her nose, the prim white regulation blouse in ribbons, skirt hanging below her knees. There had been a stunned moment before she had been seized by one of the masters, wrapped in a rug and carried at a run to the sanitorium. Ten minutes later the doctor's car had come racing up the drive, and he'd scurried into the house. Thereafter, a steel shutter of silence had been lowered. Before nightfall the police were prowling the lanes, scything the hedgerows. The more worldly-wise boys knew rape when they saw it; the younger ones shivered and cowered between the sheets.

He shouted her name, praying his eyes were deceiving him, that it wasn't Tilly, but some other girl. She lifted her head for a second, then dropped it, a second in which hope was blighted. It was Tilly, what in this horrendous moment he acknowledged to be his father's favourite child, who, like an albatross hung round his neck, it was his duty to protect. He began to run towards her. Well-briefed in the theory of sex, he hadn't too clear an idea what obscenities tramps or weirdies committed on little girls, but if Tilly had been a victim, one thing he knew for sure, his father would never forgive him. He was doomed to exist under a cloud for the rest of his life.

"Don't make such a din," Tilly snivelled, and wiped her nose on the back of her hand.

"What happened to you?" The beating of his heart created echoes of thunder in his ears, making his voice oddly high-pitched.

"I fell into a ditch. It was full of muck." She smeared away the blood seeping out of the scratch on her arm, at the mercy of such a storm of conflicting emotions they reduced her to a stoical calm. She'd been attacked by a witch who'd tried to strangle her. But she didn't propose to tell Miles, who'd fall about laughing at the idea that witches existed.

He peered into her face. "And that's all?" His voice quavered. "Nothing else? Nobody touched you?"

She jerked her head back. "I told you. I fell into a ditch."

Painful experience had developed in Miles a sense, equivalent to a built-in lie-detector, when his sister was indulging herself in grandiose fantasies. This time the lie-detector didn't seem to be working. He couldn't be certain of anything. But surely she wouldn't lie about THAT! Ashamed of a cowardice in himself, that he didn't want to know the unspeakable, he pretended to believe her, slapped a clod of dried mud from her jeans.

"If you go into the house in that filthy state, looking as if you've been knocked down by a bus, Granny will have a heart attack." He contemplated the crown of her head, sprinkled with tufts of leaves, clods of earth. "You'd better hide behind the hedge until I tell you the coast is clear. Then you can go in and clean yourself up. But you'll have to get a move on. Lunch is in twenty minutes."

On the far side of the main road, he thrust her into an angle of the garden hedge. "If there's no one in the hall, I'll open the front door, whistle, and you can make a bee-line for the bathroom." He gave her a shake. "Tilly, are you listening?"

"Yes. You'll whistle. Is there a letter from Dad?"

"No, from Mum. I put it in your room. I'll go round the back way, check on Mrs. Baker." He gazed at the miserable little object squatting in a heap, nursing her bloodied arm, yearned for words adequate to fit the occasion, for his father, his mother, then shorn of all hope of support began to run like a deer.

Mrs. Baker, detailed to keep an eye on the vegetables, didn't even glance in his direction as he sprinted through the kitchen, but in the hall, he ran straight into his grandmother's arms. "Have you found her?"

"Yes, she's okay."

A blessed relief seeped through Nelia. All that frantic, exhausting worry for nothing! Like a vision far ahead she glimpsed that distant day when her son-in-law would drive up to Srinagar, lift from her shoulders the burden of Tilly. "Where is she now?"

"Having a bath."

"At this hour!"

He nodded, keeping spoken lies to a minimum.

"Then tell her to hurry. You know what a stickler your grandfather is for punctuality. All Army officers are. It comes from eating in the Mess. Dr. Pallister is here, and he'd like some ice in his gin and tonic. Would you be a dear boy and fetch some out of the fridge?"

He carried the ice into the drawing-room, submitted with all the grace he could muster to Dr. Pallister's patronising enquiries about school, before he was free to excuse himself, escape, open the front door, and whistle. He literally propelled Tilly up the first flight of stairs, and then abandoned her.

The colonel sighted the empty chair as he painfully manoeuvred his arm crutches through the dining-room door. "Where's Matilda?"

"Just coming," Nelia soothed. "I can hear her running down the stairs."

Tilly scuttled rather than walked into the room, and with downcast eyes took the chair opposite her grandfather. Nelia beamed desperate hope. Clean white T-shirt, denim skirt, regulation sandals. Nothing to raise Reggie's blood pressure except the strands of hair dribbling water on to the table. Colonel Furston counted twelve separate drips on to the rosewood surface before he demanded, "May I enquire why you choose to appear at lunch with wringing wet hair."

"I washed it in my bath."

In a vain attempt to create a diversion, Nelia gave a merry laugh. "What an extraordinary way of shampooing it. I don't think it's a very good idea to sit there dripping water over all of us. Go and ask Mrs. Baker to give you a towel. Maybe she'll rub it dry for you."

Mrs. Baker emitted a long-suffering sigh, picked up the nearest tea-towel. "Dedicated to causing trouble, that's you." She opened the door of the still-warm oven, kicked a stool under Tilly's bottom, and began to rub. "Be the death of your poor old grandpa, you will."

The rhythm of the rubbing first soothed then boosted Tilly's ego. She won a fight with a witch! As confirmation she surreptitiously fingered the watch tucked in her pocket. But suppose the witch appeared again, trapped her in a corner, overpowered her and stole the watch from her! She meditated so long that rubbing a head that was as lifeless as a doll's, Mrs. Baker thought she'd fallen asleep. In fact, Tilly was compiling a list of hiding places for the watch, deciding which was the safest.

"Want your dinner now?"

"Yes, please."

"Better make do with kitchen company and leave your poor old grandpa in peace, eh? I spooned out some of the mousse. Thin as syrup. We'd best drink it. Your granny would have done better to let me make a fruit tart, but no, it had to be something with a fancy name."

When they'd finished, Mrs. Baker threw Tilly the half-dried tea-cloth which had been used on her hair. "Be careful how you wipe the cutlery. Smears bring your grandpa out in spots."

Tilly gave a trancelike nod. The empty disused greenhouse! It had a clinker floor. She'd dig a hole, wrap the watch in a cellophane bag, bury it under the clinker and it would be safe from the witch until her father arrived home.

*

In the dusk Anna sat on the rug and with dreamlike gestures fed the newly spurting flames with wood shavings, listening, smiling, hoarding the words that no one could hear but herself. At the sound of a car arriving, she frowned, but the frown vanished as she recognised Edmund's footsteps.

It was the serene smile on her lips, a restored inner quietude that swept him with a wave of hope that she was back to normal, the Anna he knew. "How are you?" And then, when she didn't immediately answer, added, "I worry about you."

It was an understatement in that she kept him in a permanent state of stress, absorbing too much of his mental capacity when he needed to be at the peak of his form to circumvent any mischief that filthy old drunk might be brewing. A creature of the night who maybe—or maybe not—possessed the power to land him in gaol for twenty years.

When she did not answer but held that half-provocative smile on her lips, he teased, "I suspect you've forgotten the human body needs to be fed."

"Oh, I eat." She remembered she had a bone to pick with him, a lie to expose. As though it was a treat, she hoarded it up. "I might even cook you a meal. Say an omelette and salad with a bottle of hock to wash it down."

"Perfect." He felt a sense of ease, like a reprieve, that the travesty of a woman, one moment spitting venom, the next blind and deaf to reason had returned to normal. Then, as she switched on the standard lamp he saw the scratch running from her hair-line into her forehead.

"What have you done to your forehead?"

She touched it with a finger. "I was clawed by a pocket-sized fiend. The child thief. She never left home. That was a cover-up devised by her grandparents, stage-managed by the police, with maybe a little help from you. Do you know where I found her this morning? In Bateman's Wood, hunting for any other loot on which she could lay her sticky fingers."

"What happened?"

"She made off." She laughed. "But don't worry, I shall catch up with her."

"Deacon told me that, temporarily, she'd been sent to stay with friends."

"He lied in his teeth." She turned on her heel and strode into the kitchen confounding his new hope, reviving the half-submerged pangs of unease. Her conversation during the meal was fitful, darting inconsequently hither and thither and then collapsing into silence. She separated the food on her plate into segments and then, seemingly forgot to eat them. Twice he caught her with her head slanted, a yearning nauseatingly sentimental look on her face as though she were listening to a voice that only she could hear.

He said, because she must be told, "The funeral is on Monday at two o'clock. Did you know?"

"Yes."

"All three offices will be closed from one P.M. I could pick you up at . . ."

"I'm not going." That had been Garth's order to her. The witnessing of his dead flesh and bone being lowered into a grave was not to be borne. To her it was a falsification of fact that she thrust fiercely out of her mind. She eyed his plate with exasperation. "As soon as you've finished, I'll brew some coffee. I never knew a man who finicked about with his food as you do. Either eat it or leave it."

When she'd hustled him into the sitting-room, she curled into her favourite pose, sprawled on the rug close to the wood fire, her arm draped across a chair, remarked, "I drove to the top of Lacestone Mount this afternoon."

The significance eluded him. A hill mid-way between Fern-well and Anderbridge, surmounted by a miniature Cleopatra's needle, erected to the memory of a former mayor who had bequeathed a sum of money to immortalise himself.

"You weren't at the boutique?"

"I told you. I drove up to Lacestone Mount."

"Why?"

"It's a vantage point. Oh, come on, you can't be that ignorant of local geography. It overlooks The Copse. All you need is a pair of binoculars."

A creeping coldness invaded his bones. No. 5 The Copse was the house Garth had purchased for his second wife. Split-level, surrounded by an acre of what was termed natural garden. Edmund knew the sum Garth had paid for it: £30,000. What he didn't know was the percentage of Garth's money Carol had squandered on fulfilling her childlike dream fantasies of a push-button kitchen, a swimming pool with what she called "an adjustable lid," a multiplicity of gadgets, art-deco furnishings with colour combinations that blinded the eye and other ill-assorted junk. Garth's reaction had been one of indulgent amusement. When Carol had been out of the room, he'd grinned. "Ghastly, isn't it? Take heart. In a couple of years, maybe less, she'll have outgrown it."

The sly, narrowed glance flickered over him. "They were lying side by side, practically in one another's arms, on the edge of the pool. For over an hour."

He asked a question to which he already knew the answer. "Who were?"

"Carol and lover-boy."

"You mean Tris. Tristram Weekes?"

"Is that his name!" She wrinkled her nose in distaste.

He bent towards her. "For God's sake, Anna, Carol is five months pregnant."

"By whom? Not that she's likely to tell you!" She laughed. "How does Tristram fill in his time? I don't imagine he does anything as degrading as work."

His answer was stiff, factual. "He's at Bristol University, reading economics."

"Useful, very. Teach him to do his sums."

"Anna, it's a family set-up. His mother, Mrs. Coombes' sister, died when he was a year old. His father took off, so the Coombes adopted him. Carol and Tris have known one another since they were children. It's a brother and sister relationship."

Her glance damned him for naïvety and stupidity. "How remarkably well informed you are about what you delicately term their relationship. Duped! All ready and eager to swallow any lie that little tart dishes out. So, presumably, you've been seeing her."

"Yesterday I telephoned Mrs. Coombes and asked if there was any way I could help. She said there were a few matters which her husband would like to discuss with me. I went to lunch. I didn't exchange more than half a dozen sentences with Carol. She's still on tranquillisers, and only ate a few mouthfuls of food before she left the table and went upstairs."

"After which presumably Daddy and you got down to the nitty-gritty. The value of the house, how long you estimated it would be before it was sold. And naturally he's already been in touch with old Carstairs, wheedled him into letting him read the will to make sure they're not being cheated of their rights, or rather Carol's. Oh, come on," she exploded, "you're a big boy now. I don't have to spell it out, do I?"

He snapped, "I'm not in the mood for playing guessing games."

"No guesses. Hard facts. Those two drop-outs from the human race have been lovers for months. But there was a teeny-weeny fly in the ointment. Tristram hasn't a bean, and neither has she. So what do they do? Say good-bye to luxury living, rent some squalid flat? That would hardly be in keeping with what they've become accustomed to, would it? So they put their heads together, plot and plan, wave a magic wand, and hey-presto Carol is a widow, a rich widow, with a fortune to burn!"

"Are you accusing them of Garth's murder?"

"What else?"

No words that would release her from an obsession that amounted to paranoia came to his tongue. Brutally he chose one that Anna couldn't contradict. "She is carrying Garth's child."

Hate contorted her face beyond recognition. Through clenched teeth she hissed, "All right, I'm barren. A barren woman, who can't bear a child. Go on, shout it from the house-tops."

Her hands began to shake as though with ague; to steady

them she clenched them hard one within the other. "If you believe it's Garth's child, you'll believe anything. If they didn't
kill him, who did? He hadn't an enemy in the world. Go on,
line up a list of suspects. Name them." Her voice became a
menacing whisper. "I dare you!"

Because of his inadequacy to cope with a mind run amok, he
could not speak. Alternative waves of exasperation and anger
drained him. So that he could turn his back on her, create a
small breathing space for himself, he walked to the window.
"What steps do you propose to take?"

She jeered, "I'd hardly be likely to confide in you, would I?
You can't even exercise enough pressure to bring a child thief
to justice!"

"I know Carol. I've met Tris twice. Mr. and Mrs. Coombes
are ordinary, decent people. You've no evidence they were remotely concerned with Garth's murder. If you broadcast what
you appear to believe . . ." He turned, saw her half-pitying,
half-mocking expression, and in the same moment was conscious that his thought processes had spun out of control, leaving his mind in a chaos he could not restore to order.

"You're saying I'll be labelled a jealous wife?"

He nodded, then corrected himself. "An ex-wife."

She turned her back on him, clung for support to the mantelpiece. Unexpectedly pity stung deep. He went towards her.
"Anna, all this is a kind of delusion triggered off by shock."

The flames seemed to hypnotise her. Without lifting her
eyes from them, she whispered, "She's a grubby little siren, lur-
ing men to their deaths, laughing her head off as she watches
them die."

"Anna, please!"

Like a hissing cat, she spat at him. "Get out. I've work to do.
And so have you. Make that delinquent child give back the
watch she stole."

Cravenly he went. Outside in the cooling air, he could not
fathom why he had made no attempt to soothe her, even
feigned, while her mind was crippled and incapable, to place
some credence in her wild accusations. It was not his respon-

sibility to vindicate the Coombes, prove their innocence. The police had cleared them.

It was something hidden in his soul, a vaulting pride in his handiwork of which he could not bear to be deprived even by a woman teetering on the fringe of lunacy. He recalled the drawn, ravaged face, then like a whiplash another differently shaped, inimical, yet somehow threatening and relishing the threat. Sly, knowing.

A tiny pulse of fear began to drum in his blood. She could be devious, pretend to pursue one course, while intent on another. Was she playing some kind of charade, testing him out, using Carol as bait? But she couldn't know. Couldn't, he silently screamed, as horror poured like a torrent through his mind. With a supreme effort of will he wiped away, as though with a damp rag, the self-torture to which he was subjecting himself. He drew in his breath, let it out on a sigh, steeled himself against panic.

SEVEN

Mrs. Fox-Smythe, a woman of indomitable will, incapable in her own estimation of human error, was chairwoman of a joint committee covering all the voluntary services in Anderbridge and Fernwell. In a loose-leaf note-book in her crocodile handbag was a record of every old, sick or needy man/woman. Miss Madden who came top of the list as one entitled to a visit, did not recognise Mrs. Fox-Smythe, and was reluctant to admit her.

She appeared to have slept in her clothes and her general condition had deteriorated since Mrs. Fox-Smythe had last seen her eight weeks ago. Tearful, confused, incapable of answering a simple question, when a brush salesman rang the bell, she'd panicked, stumbled up the stairs, shut herself in her bedroom.

It had taken Mrs. Fox-Smythe over half an hour—a longer ration of time than her allotment for each "case"—to learn what was troubling her: an incoherent, back-tracking story of men tapping at her windows in the night, trying to break into her garage, steal a car.

The outcome was that Police Constable Maxwell, at the desk in the front office of the police station, found himself under orders that he did not consider were within Mrs. Fox-Smythe's authority to issue. "More a case for someone from Welfare I should have said."

"Constable, I *am* head of the social services in this area. May I repeat myself? Miss Madden, an elderly woman living alone, rightly or wrongly believes she is being harassed. She is in urgent need of a boost to her morale, support from someone with authority; in simple words, a uniformed policeman. To her generation the police stand for protection, the maintenance of law and order. While I was there I inspected the locks on her doors and windows, and they are by no means burglar proof. When the police have visited her, they must contact a lock-smith, check that he does a good job."

When Maxwell's face remained wooden, she gave him an encouraging nod. "Oh, I know you're busy, with a murder case on your hands, but Miss Madden's cottage isn't on the other side of the country. No more than ten minutes' drive for one of your patrol cars. A visit from a member of the police force, a promise that you will keep an eye on the place, will set her mind at rest. I suggest you call on her this afternoon."

"You've admitted the old lady is confused, that her memory is failing. So isn't it likely she'll forget any reassurance the police give her as soon as they're out of the door?"

"It is precisely because her mind is confused, her memory unreliable that I'm asking you to send one of your men to see her. You're not being very co-operative, are you? Perhaps I'd better have a word with Superintendent Deacon."

"He's at a conference. Left orders that he's not to be disturbed. I should have thought a doctor . . ."

She waved him to silence. "Her doctor is new to the practice, aged twenty-nine, looks eighteen. In any case, I doubt very much if he would be prepared to examine the locks, or would be any wiser if he did. Rightly or wrongly, Miss Madden believes burglars are trying to break into the house at night. Oh, I accept she may be suffering from delusions, but that doesn't relieve us of the responsibility of allaying her anxiety. If we don't, she's liable to become a psychiatric case, and as you should know, there is an acute shortage of beds in that ward. The community as a whole are responsible for Miss Madden's well-being. In other words you and me, Constable."

P. C. Maxwell knew when he was beaten. Mrs. Fox-Smythe served on every bloody committee in the county, sat on the bench, knew all the nobs, lived in a Stately Home. Money and time to burn since she'd been widowed. Access to the ears of those in high places. "I'll see what I can do."

She favoured him with a gracious smile, drew on her doeskin gloves. "This afternoon? Before dark?"

"If there is a car available."

"Oh, I'm sure there will be. I'll telephone you in the morning."

*

Edmund drove slowly, mental and physical fatigue inducing a lassitude that made the slightest exertion equal to clawing his way up a precipice. Fatigue, he told himself; the effort of trying to cope with Anna's dementia. A doctor? Telephone him from home, ask him to look in on her, a visit of condolence rather than a professional one? And Anna's reaction? Unpredictable. She could refuse him entry, or put on an act that would convince the doctor there was not a thing wrong with her. Her face, rigid with malevolence one moment, the next slyly knowing, glimmered in the windscreen.

The blue and white police car parked outside the squat cottage automatically sent his foot down hard on the accelerator. For seconds he could barely see the road ahead, only the flying boundaries of the hedgerows. When he reached home, had garaged the car, he bent his head over the steering wheel. When he raised it, moisture dripped on to his hands. How much did the old bitch know? What lies was she spewing out to the police? Was she handing over the watch, telling them where she had found it? Was she describing a man whose height and face tallied with his own?

At the third attempt his key slid into the lock. Once inside, the door shut, terror released its fangs, and the tension in his body eased. Even if she produced the watch, what would it prove except that she had stolen it? And what credence would be given to a witless old woman?

For comfort he drew into his lungs the scent of polish. On the gleaming rosewood table in the alcove Lance had set a silver mug filled with roses. In every direction his eyes were presented with a sensual delight in the pride of possession.

At the end of their first meeting Lance had sucked in his

cheeks, cocked his head. "Okay, what's the objection. What have you got against me except the obvious?"

"I was thinking in terms of a woman."

"Some old slut who'd cheat you left, right and centre! Spend most of the time with her feet up, smoking and spreading ash all over the place. Lots of little notes to come home to!" He glanced around. "Tailored to fit me. Keep it spanking. Knock you up a meal occasionally. And shop. You'd be in clover."

Lance had been as good as his word. Pure gold. What amounted to an invisible man. Anna had grimaced in revulsion. "He's a homo. Flaunts the fact. People will talk. Don't you care?"

"No. He's the faithful type, so I'm given to understand."

He opened the fridge. A lamb casserole ready to heat. Fresh bread in the bin, fruit on an onyx plate. On his bed clean sheets. No notes. The waves of panic began to subside. He was a gambler, always had been—forever striding into the darkness of the unknown. And, so far he'd won, and there was no reason why he shouldn't go on winning. All it took was a cool nerve. And, as for Anna, she was temporarily—he hoped—a prisoner of her own hallucination. Time should repair her sick mind.

Exchanging his jacket for a pull-over, the image of Merle swam into his head: naked in bed, delectable, infinitely desirable, wheedling in her little-girl voice, "But what is there in it for me?"

"Me."

"But not forever."

"Nothing's forever."

"That's what I mean." With unaccustomed modesty, she grabbed her dressing-gown, said primly, "A girl has to take care of herself, doesn't she? Look to the future."

She'd expected him to plead, promise, submit to blackmail! Maybe her immature self had envisaged him sinking to his knees, begging her to marry him! Instead he'd kissed her good-bye, pressed a wad of notes into her hand. It had taken him seven years of marriage, its dissolution which had rocked his sanity, to learn that the inner centre of his being belonged to himself, that the prototype of a successful salesman of property, with an adept, persuasive tongue, two different smiles, one for men, one for women, was only surface deep. He was a natural loner, severed from the human race. And loners possessed an omnipotence that no one could topple.

He poured himself a drink, sipped half of it, decided that he needed a boost to his morale, a small interval of time that would heal his ravaged nerves. Tomorrow, Saturday, he might drive to London, spend the weekend with Eve. It was over a month since he'd visited her. Eve was a different type from Merle, a relaxed, undemanding wench, who sought no more from him than he was prepared to give.

Later, dinner eaten, china and silver washed and polished, the rooms restored to perfect symmetry, he poured himself a brandy and set about devising a pilot scheme that would put paid to any potential for harm possessed by the loony old bitch who'd temporarily thrown him off course. He began to smile, and then very faintly, to laugh.

*

Anna debated whether she should present her indictment to the police in person or in writing. She decided on the latter. She was a skilled typist with a flair for fluent, telling phrases. She first typed a rough copy, made certain corrections that Garth suggested, re-typed and checked through it, before she enclosed two copies in an envelope that should reach the recipient on Monday morning.

*

This Saturday had been a starred day in Miles's diary since before he'd left home: the day he was to spend with his best friend, Bywaters, who lived only forty miles from Anderbridge. Bywaters senior, accompanied by his son, was to pick him up at 9:30 and return him in the late evening. The occasion had, until on that never-to-be-forgotten day he'd watched Tilly climb the lane, been the high spot of the holidays. Now he was haunted by dread of a calamity that might befall Tilly while he was absent—for which he would be accounted responsible even though he was miles from Srinagar. Taking care not to smudge his newly polished shoes, he quartered the garden like a gun-dog in search of his sister. Any minute Mr. Bywaters would draw up at the curb, and to be overheard exhorting his sister to behave herself would lower him in Bywaters' esteem, since Bywaters had no sisters and was noted for maintaining his cool in a crisis. In the end he was driven to shouting her name, uttering threats.

The door of the abandoned greenhouse creaked open, and Tilly, dust-streaked, cobwebs clinging to her hair, appeared.

"What on earth are you doing in there? It's empty. It has been for years. No one goes in there. It's falling to pieces."

"It isn't empty. It's full of spiders, hundreds of them. I was rescuing one that had fallen out of its web." Also spreading uninhabited webs as camouflage over the clinker she had disturbed.

He advanced menacingly. "You've got to promise me you won't go wandering away for hours, worrying Granny. You're to stay put in the house. There'll only be the two of you and if Grandfather had a stroke, as he might, there'd be no one to help her, even to telephone for the doctor."

Her expression unperturbed, seemingly immune to conscience, triggered off a yawning doubt. Maybe it was his duty to forgo the day with Bywaters, stay home and keep guard on Tilly, be on hand to cope with any emergency. But it was too late to telephone; Bywaters, junior and senior, would be on their way. As Tilly began to slope off, he grabbed her shoulder, shook it. "Promise you won't go trespassing into woods and places where you've no right to be. That you'll stay here until I get back. Go on."

She made a perfunctory cross on her chest, shook him off, and walked sedately towards the house. Simultaneously Bywaters cried, "That's it, Dad. On the left."

*

After Miles had driven away, Nelia carried Reggie's breakfast tray upstairs. Before opening the door, she pinned a serene smile on her mouth. "Sorry, darling, I'm a bit late, but I had to have a word with Mr. Bywaters. Such a pleasant man. Young Bywaters isn't as tall as Miles and, poor boy, he's short-sighted and has to wear glasses. The two were delighted to see one another. Mr. Bywaters promised to have Miles home by eight. I thought I'd make a few snacks to have with drinks . . ."

Reggie, not taking in a word she'd said, prodded a finger at a column on the back page of *The Times*. "Read that."

"Sallenby. On Aug. 24th., suddenly, General Sir George Sallenby, aged 60, dearly loved husband of Anne."

"Oh, dear!" Nelia cast a nervous glance at Reggie. The death of a brother officer! He'd gloom over it for days, maybe weeks. "Poor Anne, I must write to her. They were such a devoted couple."

"It says no letters."

"People always do. I'll only write a short note, telling her not to reply."

His colour rising, his moustache appearing to bristle, he demanded, "Do you know what killed him? Pills! Ten a day, that's what he told me, and they didn't do him a happorth of good. Millions of pounds poured down the drain, the drug companies amassing fortunes!" He glared at the row of bottles on the dressing-table. "Throw them down the lavatory. They're nothing but slow poison."

She stroked his cheek. "Don't let your egg get cold." The anger drained away; in its place was stark fright. He was frightened of dying! Her Reggie: the bravest of the brave, and all because he'd lost an old comrade in arms he hadn't seen for ten years! She kissed his forehead, put the egg-spoon in his hand. He'd get over it, he always did, even obtained a certain satisfaction at out-living men younger than himself. But it would take a while.

He scowled at her. "The wrong people breed, live in luxury on the taxes they squeeze out of us. We're becoming a nation of scroungers and malingerers."

His attention was happily diverted from death prowling at

his heels to his favourite hobby-horse, the extortionate taxation
to which the middle-class were subjected. Nelia agreed with
every word, encouraged him to grumble. Ire was a more effec-
tive aid to digestion than self-pity. He cleared his breakfast tray
while she spread out his clothes in the order he put them on.

"Why don't you make Tilly fetch and carry for you? Do her
good to consider someone else for a change."

"She's in her bedroom. There was a letter from John. She likes
to read them by herself."

Reggie grunted disgust. He had a very low opinion of his son-
in-law.

*

Tilly was sitting on the edge of the bed, crossing out the day
that had only just begun. The postscript to her father's letter
had deflated her. He was preaching, trying, across hundreds of
thousands of miles to nudge her conscience. "Before you get
mixed up in any exciting adventures, think hard whether I'd
have said yes or no. Be honest, tell yourself the truth. And if
you think I'd have said no, work out why you don't agree, and
we'll talk about it when I get back. Don't forget Granny has a
lot of work to do looking after the two of you, and that Grandfather is often in pain. Okay?"

No, it wasn't. That horrible sneak Miles had been telling
tales. It wasn't fair. Tears of indignation spurted from her eyes.
Spying on her, when all she'd done was to help the police and
fight off the witch. For comfort she sucked Kipper's ear.

Bored, fuming at the injustice inflicted upon her, like an im-
prisoned squirrel she sought frantically all morning for a legiti-
mate means of escape. But with her grandmother never far
from her heels, there wasn't one. It was only when she was wip-
ing up the lunch dishes, inspiration flashed.

"When Daddy was in hospital having his appendix out, we
used to take him grapes, big, black ones. He said they kept him
from starving to death. When I post my letter would you like
me to buy Grandfather some grapes?"

"I think not, dear, though your grandfather is fond of hot-house grapes. I wouldn't know what time you'd be back, would I? And that worries me because while you're staying here, it is my responsibility to make sure you come to no harm."

"Harm!" Tilly echoed. "I couldn't come to any harm. I never have, never," she swore, forgetting for the moment the fight to the death with the witch. "The fruit shop is only a little way down the High Street, on *this* side of the road. I promise I'll go straight there and back. I'll run all the way. And if Grandfather likes grapes . . ." The uptilted face, the innocent smile was so tempting Nelia averted her head. Tilly sighed pathetically. "I've nothing else to do. And it would be a gorgeous surprise for him."

A respite, Nelia thought. With Reggie asleep in his chair, she could lie down on the bed for half an hour, rest her aching back. She weakened. "But you'd have to promise me you'd come straight home, not go wandering into the woods, trespassing on private property."

"Oh, I would. I would. Truly."

An empty promise, forgotten as soon as given, Nelia knew, and wondered what had become of all her loving concern, her sense of responsibility for a small, vulnerable girl child. "Very well," she said and felt as if she'd forfeited a bit of her soul.

*

Tilly skipped out of the gate, rich with a pound note for the grapes in her pocket, and the 10p left of her weekly pocket money.

As the assistant reached for a paper bag, she said, "They're a present. Can I have them in a box?"

He gave her a sour glance. "If I've any left." He found one, folded it into shape.

"And one apple, a big one."

Swinging the box from its loop of string, munching the apple, the compulsion to stroll down one side of the High Street, back along the other, monitoring shop windows was irresistible. When she reached the point where the shops ended and the countryside began, she'd turn back. She was nearly

through her apple when she sighted the familiar magenta crocheted cap ahead of her. She did a fast sprint, thrust her arm
through Miss Madden's, who, terrified, wrenched herself free,
then gave a cry of relief. "Goodness, you did give me a fright."

"I didn't mean to." Tilly tossed what remained of the apple-
core into the gutter, dangled the white cardboard box in front
of Miss Madden's nose. "I've been buying some black grapes
for my grandfather. He's a cripple."

"Oh, dear, I am sorry." She peered down into the pearl-white
triangle of Tilly's face. "Haven't you got a mother and father,
dear?"

"They're in Hong Kong. That's why I have to stay with my
grandparents." Drama built up. "They don't want me. They
hate having me."

Miss Madden looked shocked. "Oh, I can't believe that."

"It's true. They'd like it if I ran away and never came back."

Miss Madden's knowledge of children was nil. She accepted
the statement as true, and it pained her. She looked around for
a source of comfort. "Shall we have an ice-cream? Would that
be nice? I love an ice-cream cone, though my sister never ap-
proved of eating one in the street."

They sat on a bench in the pocket-sized car-park, licked in
companionable silence. Tilly broke it when the ice-cream had
sunk an inch below the biscuit. "A witch tried to strangle me,
in the woods. You know the one near your house where I found
the dead man, and where Daddy and I watched the weasel."

Miss Madden, incapable of assimilating the string of facts
presented to her, blinked. As Mrs. Fox-Smythe had discovered,
she was only capable of digesting one subject at a time. She
shook her head, waiting for inspiration. "You should tell the
police."

Tilly was non-committal. The police had let her down. "Perhaps I will."

Miss Madden stared in vague disbelief. "Did you say a
witch?"

"With fangs, finger-nails running with blood. Like a vam-
pire." Ice-cream and cone consumed, she spread her hands,

feinted a stranglehold on Miss Madden's throat. Miss Madden screamed, and a policeman checking cars, came towards them on pounding feet. "You all right, madam?"

"Of course she is." Tilly's scathing glance dismissed him. "We're only playing vampires."

"Quite all right," Miss Madden mumbled.

When he'd returned to the cars, Tilly untied the string on the box. "Would you like a grape?"

Miss Madden peered longingly at the luscious black globes, coated with bloom. "I wouldn't say no." And heard the phantom voice of Dorothea snap, "Then say, yes."

"Delicious!" They smiled contentment at one another, as Tilly reversed the bunch of grapes to hide the naked stalks.

*

"Shall I take the grapes to Grandfather?"

Despite the crust of ice-cream on her mouth, the dried runnels of juice on her chin, Tilly's smile was seraphic. Nelia who'd been on pins and needles for the last hour, peering through the window for a sight of Tilly, gazed at the unharmed child, acknowledged that she'd harried herself into miseries of dread for no reason at all. If only she could bring herself to accept Tilly's wanderlust she would be released from the anxiety that kept her in a permanent state of fright. Be at peace. Gradually, comforting, reassuring thoughts expanded in her head. Tilly was blessed with a charmed life. Such children did exist, wards of heaven so to speak. All the hours she'd spent imagining Tilly run-over, lured by a bag of sweets into a car, at the mercy of a strangler. And there was Tilly before her, guilty of no more than sucking an ice-cream cone in the street, plundering some of her grandfather's grapes.

She told herself that present-day children were so much more self-reliant than previous generations. Wasn't she an old fuddy-duddy incapable of accepting the liberties they enjoyed today? Off to camps by themselves, on day trips to France where they could easily fall overboard, but never did! She reached out for the comfort offered her, grabbed it.

"Yes, dear. But wash your face first, and put on a clean dress. Is that ice-cream on your sandals?"

"I expect so. If Rufus was here he'd lick it off."

A charmed life, Nelia whispered to herself, when Tilly had run off, closing her ears to a faint voice that warned that unsupported hope can cheat, destroy.

*

Deacon returned from the afternoon conference in a sour mood to face a pile of reports on his desk. The top one consisted of a short letter clipped to three sheets of foolscap neatly stapled, professionally typed, paragraphs inset and numbered. The gist of it absorbed, he pressed his buzzer for Warren. "Read that."

Warren flipped it over to scan the signature, skimmed through it.

"Well?"

Warren shrugged. "Middle-aged wife exchanged for a dollybird. Brand new model! Happens all the time. Since she and Rampton were divorced over two years ago, you'd think she'd have become reconciled. Apparently not. Still nursing a grievance. Remember the watch episode that earned us a broadside from Colonel Furston?"

"A watch that we haven't found!"

"That's so. We widened the area of search, but we came up with nothing. Carol Rampton still thinks he was wearing it when he drove her to her parents' home, but she can't swear to it. Frankly, she's not yet in a state to be certain of anything." He returned the stapled sheets to the desk. "No substance in it, sir. They've all been checked out. You know that. Neighbours saw Rampton and his wife drive up, greeted by Mrs. Coombes and the adopted son who'd just arrived back from a hitch-hike across Europe. Mr. Coombes reached the house around six. No evidence that he, or any other member of the family took the car out that night. Coombes is an accountant, a desk-man, swore he'd never touched a gun in his life. And I'd accept his word. The boy isn't a tearaway. Caught a dose of religion, all tied up with some cult, doesn't believe in owning anything, is of the opinion that money is the root of all evil. You know the type!"

Deacon tossed the typed pages back at him. "Have it acknowledged, say we're investigating the charges she makes. Are the Coombeses still living in the house?"

"Took off after the funeral. Mr. Coombes telephoned, said he and his wife thought the girl would be better with them. Seemed a sensible idea."

Deacon brooded. "Did she attend the funeral? The first Mrs. Rampton, I mean."

"No, sir. Big turn-out, though. Most of the locals. All the staff from the three offices. Mayor, local dignitaries, etc. No one I didn't know."

Deacon's eyes narrowed by puffy lids, fastened on his Detective Inspector. "Someone shot Rampton, murdered him." With a fist the size of a ham he thumped the desk. "Nine days ago!"

"Yes, sir."

"A little more action, wouldn't you say, for all concerned?"

"Action hasn't been lacking, sir."

"But so far no results. For instance, we've not come up with a car, any car, or van seen in the vicinity of Bateman's Wood on the night Rampton was murdered. He couldn't have crawled there himself, could he, covered his head with ivy! So who dumped him there, then drove Rampton's car into the lay-by on the Colteshall Road?"

"We don't know, sir." He half turned, then reversed and faced Deacon. "There's an old lady, a Miss Violet Madden who lives practically opposite Bateman's Wood. Immediately after the discovery of the body she was interviewed by Detective Constable Jones. Elderly, sir, muddled in her head. Bit senile. Refused at first to open the door more than a crack. Was incapable, apparently, of answering questions, became distressed, and eventually Jones ticked her off the list."

"Well?"

"Yesterday Mrs. Fox-Smythe called in to express concern

about the old lady. The usual story: living alone, not able to look after herself, still knocked off balance by the death of her sister a few months ago. Mrs. Fox-Smythe insisted—and you know what she's like when she gets her teeth into anything—that Miss Madden was in need of support from the police. Among other things, she wanted the locks checked. Apparently the old lady is convinced burglars are trying to break in. I sent Simpson, who's got a nice touch with old ladies, along to see her. His report is being typed now. It seems she told him she saw a car. She'd fallen asleep downstairs and was woken up by what she thought was her cat crying to be let in. She ran out into the road, the car swerved to avoid her, and had a bit of a job reversing out of the ditch before it drove on."

Deacon glared impatience. "Well, go on."

"Thought there might be something in it, but it turns out that the cat had been run-over a week previously. Simpson checked with the jobbing gardener who works for her occasionally. He buried the cat and remembers the exact day because the old girl was in a state of collapse when he arrived."

"And she doesn't, of course, remember the number of the car, make or colour! Not that it matters if the cat was killed a week before Rampton was murdered."

"In Simpson's opinion she wouldn't know a Mini from a Rolls-Royce. Thinks the car was grey, but she did remember the last numeral on the number plate. Four. She'd noted it because it was the number of the house she'd lived in before she and her sister moved to the Tied Cottage. I agree it's a slim chance. But it might be worth checking."

"One numeral! A car swerving into a bank when Rampton had another week to live!" He gave one of his famous snorts of contempt. "We've no time to waste on dead ends. Concentrate, man. Use your wits."

"We have concentrated, sir. But so far we haven't got any results."

"Then someone better produce some, hadn't they, or we look like getting our knuckles rapped. Senile old women, cats, a car that might or might not be grey on the road when Rampton was hale and hearty! Forget it, get down to basics. Who had a grudge against Rampton, was better off when he was dead? Try that out on some of the so-called geniuses that Headquarters have off-loaded on to us."

EIGHT

On Monday morning Edmund, having driven from Knights-
bridge to the office, telephoned Anna at the boutique. The visit
to Eve had had a soothing effect, deadened the shock of the
police car stationary outside the old cretin's gate. He'd spent
the journey devising a plan that would put paid to her little
chats with the law, but he still had to verify a few facts before
he could go ahead. Thereafter, it was a matter of precision-tim-
ing in which he, rightly, counted himself an expert.

The bogey was Anna, the nag of unease she roused in him, so
that he was forever checking on her. Love—hate—he'd never
realised how terrifyingly interchangeable they were. A constant
switching from one to the other. Over the weekend he'd dallied
with the idea of persuading her to take a holiday. Why not
Rome, a city she loved, where she could browse among the
collections? Granted, they were way beyond the purses of her
matronly clientele, but there were the accessories, costume-jew-
ellery, knick-knacks that she could dangle tantalisingly before
her more fashion-conscious customers.

Surprising him, her voice was normal, though brisk, suggesting she had no time or inclination to waste on chat. He made
no reference to the funeral, did not so much as enquire how
she was, but suggested dinner at Pharaoh's in Fernwell, the best
eating-house in the town. She accepted without a quibble and
he promised to pick her up at seven.

Though the front door was open, and he called her name,
there was no response. Not downstairs, not up. Where the hell
was she? After a two-months' scorching heat-wave the weather

had broken. The evening was overcast, chilly, with an intermittent drizzle, not conducive to being outdoors.

He found her sitting on a teak seat on the circle of paving
that enclosed the lily pool, cradling an armful of white roses,
wearing a limp, nondescript dress, the hem of which had been
trailed through the damp grass, and clung, bedraggled, to her
ankles, unheeding of the temperature or the click of his footsteps.

"Anna!"

In slow motion she turned her head, gave him the trance-
look that set alarm bells ringing in his head.

"Anna!" This time he shouted, needing to reassure himself
that she could speak and walk, wasn't locked in some form of
catalepsy. She rose, holding the blossoms close, casting a lingering eye over the three formal beds. Crimson, peach, white.
Only the white rose bushes had been plundered.

She bent over the blooms, touching them with her lips. "I
must put these in water before we go."

She collected a black vase from the kitchen and with silent
absorption arranged each stalk, standing back to examine her
handiwork, bending one rose here, lowering another deeper
into the water, until she was satisfied with the symmetry.

His patience snapped. "Alexis doesn't guarantee to hold res-
ervations after eight."

She ignored his protest. "There!" She caressed an unfurling
bud. "Garth's favourite roses. He always wanted snow-white
roses in all the beds, said they'd be perfect against the background of the yews. And he was so right. I'll have the other two
beds dug out in the autumn, replanted with white. Okay, I'm
ready."

"Shouldn't you have a wrap over that thin dress?"

"Oh, for goodness' sake don't fuss. We're not on our way to
the Ritz. Anyway, you can drop me at the door before you park
the car."

When Alexis put the *carte* in her hand, she graciously passed
it back to him. "You choose, Alexis. Paté to start with and then

one of your specialities. Surprise us! And that goes for the wine too."

"And you, Mr. Lang? As Madame says?"

"Yes."

"An *apéritif?*"

"Please. Two large gin and tonics."

"Not for me, Alexis. I'll wait for the wine."

Edmund stared at a face that had reshaped itself into a mask of demureness grotesque in a middle-aged woman. Anna who drank like a fish and always preceded a meal with three double gins. His mind slipped back, framed a vignette: Anna holding out her glass to be refilled for the fourth time, Garth mildly demurring, Anna rising, stalking to the drinks table and helping herself. The truth leapt at him, chilling his flesh. She was acting a part drawn from the past. Forswearing spirits to appease, placate a dead man! Probably on some occasion, in this restaurant, Garth, who was no gourmet, had handed over responsibility for choosing the food to Alexis. Now Anna was play-acting the rôle of a devoted and pliant wife—which she'd never been. For a moment shock and revulsion sickened him.

She did not speak until Alexis poured the wine, then gave Edmund a conspiratorial smile. "Drink up. This evening is by way of being a celebration."

"Of what?"

"Or to be more precise, the eve of a celebration." Though Anna had anticipated a summons from Deacon that day, she told herself that her statement would require careful cross-checking before a bumbling, dim-witted over-weight police officer on the verge of retirement committed himself to action. He would telephone her in the morning.

His voice sharpened. "Must you talk in riddles?"

She laughed. "It shouldn't be a riddle to you. I've put all the facts, chapter and verse, before Deacon. On paper. That way it will have more impact. I shall be seeing him tomorrow."

"The Coombeses!"

She nodded. "Killers, with or without an accessory before or after the fact."

He felt his temper that normally he was able to control, bubble, explode within him. "You've no evidence, not a shred. You're making a bloody fool of yourself, worse, a laughing stock." For a moment he was confused, unable to understand why, once again, he was squandering precious nervous energy on striving to bring Anna to her senses. The answer was there, waiting. Any imbalance of mind in her reflected on him, evoked the unspeakable memories of the psychiatric ward that he kept buried in some secret cavern, and which now threatened to burst out of their prison.

"Evidence! I've all I need. Work it out for yourself. They'd everything to gain, nothing to lose provided they weren't found out. That baby isn't Garth's. It's lover-boy's. Its conception probably triggered off the murder. You don't imagine that long-haired play-boy intends to work for his living, do you? And the weekly dole wouldn't keep Baby-doll in luxury, would it?" She smiled sweetly at Alexis. "That duck looks delicious. The paté was out of this world."

When Alexis was out of earshot, he demanded, "What precisely did you mean by accessory?"

"They exist, come in very handy to work out a ground-plan; do a cover-up."

He wanted to flay her with his tongue, beat some sanity into her, but the restaurant was small, the tables close together. He'd already caught curious glances reaching out in their direction. He cast his own downward, put food into his mouth with no consciousness of what he was eating.

She proceeded to humour him. "Have you seen Eve lately?"

He said no. She gave a dramatic sigh of forbearance at his sulky manner, and thereafter made no effort to sustain the conversation. Once or twice she assumed the pose he'd observed before: that half tilt of the chin, as though she were listening to a voice inside her head. It both revolted and unnerved him. Communication with the dead, if that was her ploy, was a spooky game played by credulous fools that eventually landed them in a home for the insane. Was that to be Anna's fate? The word accessory stuck like glue in his head. Meaningless, he told himself, an off-shoot of her mania for revenge. He stared blank-eyed at the white starched table-napkin in his lap overwhelmed by an emotion that was equally balanced between racking pity and a storm of alarm.

Without mentioning the trip abroad—that was a dead duck —he drove her home, escorted her to the door. As he stepped back her hand flew out to clench his wrist in a pincer grip. "How do you know? Why are you so sure?"

"What do you mean?"

"I mean, how do you know that Carol and lover-boy didn't murder Garth?"

"I told you. There's no evidence, not a shred. The police have cleared them."

Her voice dropped to a whisper that was more intimidating than a scream. "Liar." Her glance minutely examined every inch of his face. "You've forgotten that I always know when you're lying. I can see into your head, read your thoughts. I always could." She released his wrist, flung it from her, slammed the door in his face.

He sat in the car for a length of time he couldn't measure. Sifting, sorting, ranging fact against fact. Tracing to its root every step he had taken, every word spoken since the moment when he'd replaced the lid on the well, walked back to the house. There was no way in which she could have gleaned a shred of evidence. No way. Even an antenna as sensitive as Anna's was incapable of uncovering his trail, spreading it out for the world to read.

He reversed the car, and to remove the last grit of uncertainty, he re-examined the background of the divorce. Anna's vehement refusal to countenance it had endured for months, to the accompaniment of sulks and hysterical denunciations. Then suddenly, she'd given way. Yet if she'd been so bitter, she could have withheld the freedom for which Garth pleaded for another year.

It had been Garth, not Anna, who'd told him of the final settlement. "It's a wretched business. I'm not proud of my part in it. But the situation is untenable, has been for years. Any problems that arise for Anna, I'll do my utmost to solve. And the settlement should maintain her in comfort for the rest of her life. I hope I don't have to say that the divorce will make no difference to our relationship, either personally or professionally."

When he'd offered Anna his sympathy, she'd shrugged it off as a non-event. "Garth hankers after a baby-doll to call his own. He's welcome to her." Thereafter she'd never mentioned Garth's name. Which had led him to assume she'd accepted the inevitability of the divorce, put it behind her. And yet, for over two years the merciless craving for revenge had been feeding on itself, sustaining a vitriolic jealousy.

. He found it inconceivable that he'd neither seen nor sensed the metamorphosis of someone whose nature he'd have sworn was as transparent to him as his own. Or was it the shock of Garth's death that had triggered off a personality change? Not to know was a form of anguish that belittled him in his own eyes.

Deliberately he channelled his thoughts into the immediate future, examined the sky. The moon was full, over-bright. To rid himself of the old hag he needed cloud, preferably intermittent, drifting.

On the threshold of the sitting-room he stopped abruptly. So faint that only a committed non-smoker would have detected it, the odour of cigarette smoke assailed his nostrils. Lance didn't smoke; anyway, this wasn't his day.

Switching on the lights, he walked through to the kitchen, saw with his eyes the unbelievable: the back door parted two inches from its frame, the key protruding. For a minute his lids closed in total rejection of a fact that could not be true. Then, like a sleep-walker, he went forward to confirm by touch the evidence confronting him, twisting the key six times in its slot to prove there had been no forced entry.

He turned away, sick and shaking, his confidence undermined, tracking back through every second of time before he'd left the cottage on Saturday afternoon.

One exit, one re-entry through the back door and the lean-to

porch, when he'd carried grapefruit skins, an empty wine bottle, dregs of salad wrapped in newspaper to the dustbin. As
though it were his *doppel-ganger* he watched himself locking
and bolting the back door, then as he swabbed down the sink
unit picking up a basin of scraps of fat, half a stale loaf for the
birds. He'd re-opened the door and from the porch thrown out
the fat and bread, watched as they'd fought, seen the starlings
win. Simultaneously there'd been a rapping on the sitting-room
window. He'd turned to see Geoff Francis's face pressed against
the glass, made grotesque by the flattened nose, the grinning
clown's mouth. Groaning, Geoff was an insufferable bore, he'd
walked through to the front door, to let him in. Still wearing
his grass-stained cricketing clothes, Geoff, though they were no
more than acquaintances, had clapped him on the shoulder.
The Anderbridge team had won. First time this season. He'd
scored a half-century. So what about a celebration drink at the
Crown and Anchor?

Edmund, time running out on him, refused. Geoff, with a
good few pints of beer inside him, slumped into a chair. It took
Edmund twenty minutes to get him launched on his feet.
Numbed, he waited for the next sequence: locking and bolting
the back door. However hard he coerced and hounded his
memory he failed to summon that image to mind. In its place
was a blank, as though a piece of film had been snipped out.
Then, the film rolling again, he saw himself hurrying into the
bedroom to pick up his over-night bag, checking his car keys,
hearing the slam of the front door, double-locking it, hurrying
to back the car out of the garage, closing the door, and then
speeding away, cutting through to the motor-way, lopping off
seconds because he'd be the best part of an hour late arriving at
Eve's flat.

An aberration of the mind? A lapse of memory as though a
fragment of his life had been filched from him? Yet his memory was a perfect instrument that had never faltered until now
when he'd been cheated by a weakness in himself he had not
known existed.

Now, with open doors, the night air flowing in, the taint of cigarette smoke was no longer detectable. But it had existed, proof that someone had wandered at will through his house, touched his possessions, defiled them. He began opening drawers, checking cabinets, shelves and wardrobe. No object was missing or displaced. The two five-pound notes he tucked under the lining paper in his desk drawer for an unexpected emergency were still there. His clothes were draped over hangers in their usual regimented order. Such private papers as he kept at home: insurance policies, television licence, clips of bills and receipts were in their customary pigeon-holes. No food had been stolen from the refrigerator.

He flirted for a moment with the idea that the scent of tobacco had been an hallucination, but he knew he had not been guilty of deceiving himself. The slightest whiff was obnoxious to him. A casual visitor, come to beg a favour, make a telephone call? Unlikely. All his contacts with neighbours were strictly formal: He had never entered their houses, they had not been invited into his. That led him to a final possibility he had been dodging. A police officer, maybe two. He saw them thrusting their prying lumpish fingers into his pockets, turning over papers, feeling under the layers of underwear, and experienced physical nausea. He fought it off. There'd been no satisfaction for prying eyes and fingers. The well had swallowed its secrets for all time. The house had nothing to reveal. If the police had pawed over his possessions, their time had been wasted, their hopes blighted.

Normally his dreams were vivid, precisely delineated, neatly rounded off with no dragging ends, evidence that, even in sleep, he exercised control over his sub-conscious.

He woke drenched in sweat, his pyjama jacket rucked in a cord round his throat, breath laboured, heart pounding. He tore off the damp jacket, flung back the bed-covers. A dream out of a horror movie from which his screams had awakened him. There was an ache in his throat, an echo of hysteria in the air.

He'd been walking, as he sometimes did on a Sunday morning, along the right of way that led across fields and wound through occasional thickets. At the sound of steps behind him he'd wheeled, expecting to see one of his neighbours, and been confronted by the filthy old crone advancing towards him, near enough now for him to see the bright slits of malevolence between her wrinkled eyelids.

He quickened his pace, mystified as to how a half-crippled old woman had covered not less than two miles of rough ground that separated her from the nearest habitation. His strides lengthened until he was running, oblivious of the thin branches that whipped his face, the ruts that tripped him. She was gaining on him. As he turned in panic, raised a protective arm, a hand clutched his shoulder, and the two of them were wrestling, the obscene claw-hands reaching for a stranglehold on his throat, screeching, "Murderer . . . murderer!"

He sat on the edge of the bed, his head locked in his hands, struggling to convince himself that what he'd suffered was no more than a nightmare: a horror scene that had no substance except in some crevice deep in his sub-conscious. He plugged his ears to hold at bay the echoes of the night she'd screeched obscenities at him. Then a brain cell that had lain dormant ticked into life, touching off a memory. Among the obscenities she'd screamed had been a man's name, repeated time and time again. He had to wait five minutes before it came to his tongue. Sammy. Who the hell was Sammy? He'd assumed she lived alone. He couldn't conceive that any human being would willingly share a dwelling with a demented vagabond who wandered the roads by night. Two days earlier, admittedly, he'd glimpsed a man cutting the front hedge—taken him for an odd-job man who'd go home at night.

But he had no firm proof, and it became imperative he established that the man didn't sleep in the cottage. He bathed, dressed, drank three cups of strong, sweetened black coffee to steady his nerves. There were two routes he could take from home to the office. Since the day he'd seen her holding the watch to her ear he'd alternated them so that, if the old bitch was wandering around, the car would not become familiar to her. This morning he took the shorter route that would take him past her cottage. Luck was with him: ahead a juggernaut, hauling itself snail-like up the incline. Instead of passing it, he hung on, even falling a little behind as he drew level with the cottage.

From his crawling car he saw the front door was open, the postman on the doorstep; on the other side of the open door, stood a grey-haired man in shirt-sleeves, a dog at his feet. As the postman turned, he heard him cry, "So long, Mr. Pritchard. Give my . . ." the rest was lost.

A man *inside* the house with a dog! The same man he'd seen cutting the hedge. So what was his status? Lodger? Relation? Friend who lived in the house?

During the remainder of the drive his brain was at the mercy of jets of panic. Yet, when he walked into the office the steps he proposed to take to discover whether or not the nemesis who dogged his heels lived alone, were precisely delineated in his head.

Audrey, over the years, by a process of osmosis had acquired an encyclopaedic knowledge of the inhabitants of the small town. Edmund glanced up from his desk. "The garden's getting out of hand. Do you happen to know any odd-job man who's free a day a week to mow, weed, do some general tidying up?"

She glanced disapprovingly over her spectacles. "I thought you enjoyed working in the garden. Cooped up all day, an outdoor hobby is what you need."

He curbed his irritation at her bossiness. "I have no intention of giving up gardening. I merely need a little temporary assistance; a hand with some of the heavy work. But if you don't know of anyone, forget it."

"Oh, I can find you someone, provided you're prepared to pay the current rate for the job. Five pounds a day. Old men prepared to tip their caps for a pound are extinct."

"Well, do your best, there's a good girl. And make it as snappy as you can. The garden is a shambles."

Mollified by the "girl," she giggled. "I daresay I can come up with a few possibles. Universal Aunt, that's me."

At the door, he called over his shoulder, "Oh, I did hear of one man, Pritchard I think his name is. But I can't contact him because I don't know where he lives."

At half-past four she put before him a list with four names, three telephone numbers and one address.

"The first two are experienced gardeners but they're fully booked up. You'd probably have to make do with odd hours in the evening. I can vouch for Mr. Clapham, he works for a neighbour of mine, does a first-class job, but he's on holiday for a fortnight, so I've no means of knowing until he gets back whether he has any free time. Your Mr. Pritchard, I'm afraid, has a poor record. Unreliable, comes when he feels like it, stays away when he doesn't. Lives in a caravan at the bottom of River Lane, and as his only transport is a bike, he might not be keen to take the job. Clapham would be the best bet, though he does tend to go down with bronchitis in the winter. Still, you wouldn't need him much then, would you?"

"No, I wouldn't." He thanked her.

She gave him a pert flirtatious glance. "Always glad to oblige the boss, even though he doesn't look quite himself today."

So the guardian with a dog wasn't a lodger in the cottage, but with his own quarters well over three miles away. His luck was holding. He spent half an hour juggling with time sequences, jotting down code words that would have been incomprehensible to anyone but himself on a scrap of paper which he tucked in his wallet. Like a game of chess. If you made the right moves, kept one jump ahead of your opponent, you couldn't lose.

*

The only letter for Anna was an electricity bill. Harnessing her impatience, she decided that Deacon was more likely to telephone than write, and throughout the morning she waited in her box-like office for his summons. By two o'clock her patience was drying up. By 3:30 gusts of resentment at his delaying tactics sent her sprinting to her car to pick up the afternoon post which would be waiting at home. Two circulars and a buff foolscap envelope. She ripped it open. Three lines formally thanked her for her letter, which was being dealt with. The signature was a wavering line she couldn't even decipher.

She grabbed the phone, demanded to speak to Detective Superintendent Deacon. The answering voice, so patently young she marvelled its owner had been let out of school, formally requested her name. Her tapping foot kept count of the seconds before the treble voice informed her that Chief Superintendent Deacon was not in the station. Could he be of any assistance?

"No. When will he be back?"

"I'm afraid I can't say exactly."

"Then inexactly."

The young voice was unable or unwilling to commit itself. Anna hung up.

*

Deacon and Warren walked side by side up the flight of steps into the station. As he opened the door to his office, Deacon gave the younger man a sour look. "And get cracking. Hot up the pace. Murderers don't vanish in a puff of smoke. A few heads will start to roll if we don't soon get our hands on the villain who murdered Rampton."

W.P.C. Edwards, a trim brunette, was arranging letters for signature on his desk. "There's a Mrs. Rampton asking to see you, sir. She's been in the waiting room for half an hour and she's threatening to stay there until you agree to see her. About a statement she says she sent to you."

Deacon emitted a sound that was a combination of a sigh and a grunt. "Better wheel her in." He glanced at his watch. Ten minutes' soothing platitudes, larded with the charm he was capable of exerting when he chose, and he'd have her out of the station. "Oh, and bring in two cups of tea."

He walked to the door to greet Anna, shook her hand and favoured her with an avuncular smile, simultaneously registering that she was teetering on the verge of hysteria, literally falling apart at the seams. Tricky, but he'd dealt with worse. May Travers, for instance, when her lover had been jailed for beating her to pulp, had tried to run a flick knife between Deacon's ribs. Women, the most unpredictable beings on God's earth! He reflected smugly on his own wife, passive, ready to comply with any suggestion that fell from his lips, though admittedly no oil painting.

He retained Anna's hand between his own for a few seconds, guided her to a chair. "Mrs. Rampton, very good of you to send me that detailed statement. Most admirably put together, if I may say so. Quite a masterpiece." He smiled commendingly at the haggard face, the colour of old cheese, allotted ten minutes to the task of placating her before he eased her out.

With an effort Anna controlled her shaking mouth. "But what action do you intend to take? They're guilty, both of them, of premeditated murder."

The door opened. "Ah, Penny, thank you. A cup of tea is always welcome." He sipped, waited until Penny had closed the door, then bent across the desk, said solemnly, "Rest assured, Mrs. Rampton, we'll investigate your allegations. Check every line of your statement. In fact, we are in the process of doing that right now."

She wailed, "They should be under arrest, locked up."

He pursed his lips, gave her a half-rueful smile. "Judge's rules, Mrs. Rampton, very complex. And we have to keep to the letter of the law, more's the pity."

Anna thumped her clenched fist on his desk. "For all you know they might be on a plane to South America, or to some banana republic from which they can't be extradited. Murderers going free! And you sit there and smile, drinking tea, doing damn-all. Not caring a hoot."

He aped sympathy. "Mrs. Rampton, I do understand how you feel. It's a natural reaction in the circumstances. But I do assure you that they are being kept under constant surveillance, no question of them getting away, and if they are guilty, they will be taken into custody."

"If?" she screamed. "There is no if . . ." For a second she looked dazed, as if she couldn't remember where she was. She mumbled, "Jet planes, ships, hovercraft . . ."

With a barely perceptible movement he eased his cuff higher. Eight minutes. He continued in a soothing sing-song, "You really must not distress yourself, Mrs. Rampton. I give you my solemn promise that we are not dragging our feet. The guilty will be brought to . . ."

Like a petulant child she burst out, "You never even found my husband's watch . . . made that thieving child give it back. You took no action at all, allowed her not only to steal it but to keep it. My husband's most precious possession."

By that time Deacon had pressed what was known as the panic button under the desk that brought W.P.C. Edwards tapping on the door. "I'm sorry, sir, but the Chief Constable wants a word with you, rather urgently, I'm afraid."

Deacon stood up, reached for Anna's hand, eased her on to her feet. "Mrs. Rampton, I must ask you to believe there is a considerable body of men, highly trained police officers working fourteen, sometimes sixteen hours a day to lay hands on the man who murdered your ex-husband." He patted her shoulder. "We'll catch him. Never doubt that. I'll be in touch as soon as there are any developments. Meanwhile, W.P.C. Edwards will see you to your car."

W.P.C. Edwards' hand firmly cupped Anna's elbow. "This way, Mrs. Rampton."

Unreachable, in some dark labyrinth of consciousness was another horror, to do with Edmund, a terrible suspicion that she struggled not to believe. Suddenly, as though her ears had been plugged, she was aware of a thunderous silence. Garth, Garth, she whispered . . . But there was no answer, only an ice-cold loneliness. Gradually the truth welled up in her: she'd failed him, and hope lost, he'd retreated into the mists of eternity. Somehow she had to coax him back.

NINE

In a stupor of boredom, Tilly padded round the garden like a prisoner in an exercise yard, with her gaoler, Miles, squatting outside the front door. To pay him back she leant over the gate, fiddled with the latch, and when she heard him behind her, shouted in his face, "Stop shadowing me. It's bad manners, and you're a rotten sleuth. Anyway, I can run faster than you," and to prove it she raced to the greenhouse, shut herself inside.

Upstairs as Nelia laid out Reggie's best grey suit, selected his tie, socks, shirt, he asked, "Have you told the children we shan't be in to lunch?"

"Miles but not Tilly. I'll explain to her when I go downstairs. She won't mind, you know. She gets on like a house on fire with Mrs. Baker, and I've left lunch ready. We have to be home by half-past three because Mrs. Baker has to take her youngest child to the dentist." Her voice turned anxious. "Darling, you do feel up to it, don't you?"

"Of course I do; stop fussing. Always enjoy a chin-wag with old Bernard, and you and Julia will be in your element having a good gossip."

Bernard Layton and Reginald Furston had, literally, fallen over each other on their first day at prep school, and clung to one another for survival. Having lost touch for nearly half a century they had discovered that in their retirement they lived within ten miles of one another. It had been Bernard, with his obsession for a neatly partitioned life, everything pinned firmly into place, who had suggested they should lunch together on quarter days: a ritual date that, with a few lapses, they had maintained for five years.

Nelia, treading sedately downstairs, clad in her best jersey two-piece, hatted, gloves in hand, called to Tilly, "Mrs. Baker will be giving you lunch today."

"Why? Where are you going?"

"To lunch with two old friends. We'll be back before Mrs. Baker leaves." Miles materialised behind Tilly. She gave a tut of exasperation. "For healthy, intelligent children, how you two do moon around! Why not set up the badminton net or play croquet instead of just wandering aimlessly about? Children these days have no initiative." She smiled at them to remove the sting from her strictures. "And be nice to Mrs. Baker. Save her all the trouble you can. She wasn't feeling quite herself on Monday."

Mrs. Baker felt far from well, down in the doldrums of what she called "her blues." What's more, her ankles were bulging over her shoes, and she had a corn on the ball of her foot that was murder.

She viewed the reunion, with slaps on the shoulder between the two old men, cheek kisses between the women done up to the nines, with a jaundiced eye, begrudging them the gleaming Bentley parked outside the gate. It was all right for some people, gadding around in luxury cars, money to burn!

Tilly tucked her arm under Mrs. Baker's elbow, wheedled, "We could have fish and chips for lunch, couldn't we?"

"No." Mrs. Baker was in an uncompromising mood. "Your gran's made a steak and kidney pie and there's apples and custard for afters." With her husband on short-time, her housekeeping money cut by a third, she added self-righteously, "Waste not want not."

It was a dismal, silent meal with both children picking at their food—Nelia had a heavy hand with pastry. "What you two need is to go hungry!" Mrs. Baker snatched the plates away, added darkly, "You should think of the millions who go to bed with no food in their bellies."

Tilly, the last fork wiped, nipped through the kitchen door,

Miles hard on her heels. Mrs. Baker grabbed her arm. "And just where are you off to?"

"The loo, and tell Miles not to follow me, it's rude."

"And then out on a ramble round the town, giving your poor old gran a heart attack when she comes back and finds you've disappeared!" Mrs. Baker fancied there was a hammering in her chest that suggested she was in for another bout of palpitations. She released Tilly, gave her a shove. "Well, I can't chain you to a post." Longing only to get her aching feet up, she loaded the responsibility on to Miles. "It's your job to keep an eye on your sister, see she doesn't get up to any mischief. So watch her."

"Don't you dare," Tilly screeched, racing for the top floor.

"I wouldn't have to if you didn't fall into ditches, get yourself filthy, invent whopping lies."

She slammed and locked the bathroom door. Alongside her compulsion to escape from prison was a yearning for a sympathetic ear tuned to listen because no one in Srinagar ever heard a word she said. But Miss Madden would, and Mr. Pritchard if he was there. And there was Nell, forgiven now for snapping a rabbit's neck. She examined the oblong of the bathroom, found the only exit apart from the door was a slit-window fifteen feet above the ground. She eased back the bolt on the door, opened it an inch and squinting saw Miles's hang-dog face. She jauntily by-passed him. "I'm going to write my letters, and I shall lock my bedroom door."

It had become an exhilarating game, a duel of wits she was determined to win. Pay him back for bragging about Bywaters, sucking up to Grandfather.

She opened the bedroom window, swung herself out on the sill, and without a qualm slid down the pipe, landed on the shed roof, grasped the branch of the apple tree, heard it creak and jumped wildly. She landed on the grass, winded, a rip in her pants and ankles that were numb. Five minutes later she was through the gate, out on the road, victory hers, leaving Miles keeping guard on someone who wasn't there. Only coppers in her purse, she was limited to a packet of chewing gum, which did nothing to assuage her hunger. She hoped Miss Madden would have another cake.

Treading circumspectly, peering forward, glancing back, she trod on the grass verge, her footsteps near soundless, playing a game of witch-hunting. But no witch materialised, and when she'd climbed the gate, sat on the bank, there was no flying glimpse of the weasel. Suppose he'd died! Desolation swept over her. For solace she drew into her mind a picture of the big calendar. Only five uncrossed days left. She saw the car driving up to the gate of Srinagar, her outflung arms and her father's slotting into one another. After she'd told him all about finding the dead man, being attacked by a witch, not being able to find the weasel, she'd give him his present.

The front door of the Tied Cottage was ajar: two voices audible, one Miss Madden's, that mumbled, and the other high-pitched, schoolmarmy, reminding Tilly of Miss Wingate who strove to implant the rudiments of simple mathematics into Tilly's head. "If only you'd concentrate," she pleaded.

"As Mrs. Fox-Smythe explained to you, you're eligible for a Home Help. You mustn't look upon it as charity. It's the responsibility of every community to support its elder citizens. You're entitled to have one for two hours three days a week. It would probably be Mrs. Benson, an extremely capable young woman. You two would get on like a house on fire. With her help and Meals on Wheels, why you'd be in clover, no worries at all. What do you say?"

"No thank you," Violet mumbled. "I can manage for myself."

Miss Madden's head began shaking from side to side as it did when she was about to cry. Tilly, naturally resistant to discipline, flew to the rescue of a fellow-sufferer who was being bullied. She stationed herself by Miss Madden, gripped her hand, and outstared the Social Service visitor.

"Who are you?"

"My friend," Miss Madden spoke up. "She helps me. I don't need anyone else, thank you."

The Social Service visitor's glance skimmed the littered table, the spilt food, Miss Madden's slippers to one of which a caramel adhered, the accumulation of ashes in the grate. "But you haven't helped Miss Madden lately, have you?"

"My grandfather's been ill. He nearly died," Tilly improvised. "But he's getting better, so I'll be able to help Miss Madden now."

"How old are you?"

"Eleven," Tilly lied.

"Good gracious, you are a shrimp, aren't you!" She rose, addressed Miss Madden, enunciating distinctly in case the old lady was deaf—most of them were. "Now, I want you to think over my suggestions, Miss Madden. You certainly need someone to give you a hand in keeping the house in order. I don't imagine you enjoy getting down on your knees to light the fire, do you? And you probably find it exhausting to change the sheets on your bed. With Mrs. Benson here for two hours three times a week, you wouldn't have those chores to cope with. And with nourishing hot meals you'd find your general health would improve. Then, there's always the danger, if a house isn't kept scrupulously clean it will be infested with mice and other vermin. And we wouldn't like that to happen, would we!"

Miss Madden mutely shook her head.

"I'll check through Mrs. Benson's schedule and tell you which days she can come to you. Thank goodness, the police have checked your locks, replaced those that were faulty. You can feel quite safe now." She ignored Tilly, gave Miss Madden a brisk, encouraging nod. "I'll be seeing you soon."

"Wasn't she bossy?" Tilly said, casting her eyes in vain over the general litter in search of a cake. The only eatable in sight was a small plate of broken biscuits. She helped herself to two halves.

Standing nibbling, she stared at Miss Madden's bright pink scalp shining through the meagre strands of lank greasy hair, the tears oozing down her cheeks. "The impertinence!" She half choked in indignation. "In my own home. Dorothea would never have allowed her inside the door."

"She can't make you have the house cleaned, and if you

don't want to see her you can lock her out. Pretend you're not in."

Miss Madden produced from her sleeve a begrimed handkerchief, blew her nose. "Saying my house was dirty! If there was one thing Dorothea couldn't abide it was nosy-parkers." She glanced uneasily at Tilly. "It isn't dirty, is it?"

"Not very. Just a bit crumby. I'll clear the table, wash the cups and plates, and then make us some tea. Is there any cake?"

"In the blue tin, with a picture of the old king on the lid."

Tilly made three journeys to collect the dirty crockery, rinsed a couple of cups under the tap, put them to drain on the greasy board. Her mother would have chided, "You don't call those clean, do you? Use the washing-up liquid." Only there wasn't any. And the tin with the picture of George V on the lid was empty except for a few mouldy crumbs adhering to the rim.

As Tilly put the cup of tea—she hadn't bothered with a saucer—into Miss Madden's hand, her face that seemed to have shrunk in the night peered upward into Tilly's. "He came again. I heard him. He was trying to find a way in."

"Who?"

"A man, tapping at the windows, peering in."

"Well, he won't find the watch. I buried it in the greenhouse. It's a super hiding-place. No one would think of looking for it there. And it won't get damp or scratched because I wrapped it in cellophane, and I spread spiders' webs across the clinker, but only old webs, not ones with spiders living in them."

Miss Madden's hand shook, sending some of the tea on to her lap. Tilly mopped it up. "Why don't you ask Mr. Pritchard to hide in the hedge and jump on him?"

Miss Madden straightened her shoulders, sat bolt upright, repeated a precept from the Gospel according to Dorothea, "I'm not one to beg favours."

"Well, unless he came down the chimney he can't get in now you're all locked up, can he?"

Miss Madden peered into the corners of the room. "He's one

of those bully-boys who pestered me to sell them my sister's car. Now he's trying to steal it."

"But there's a padlock on the garage. The police put it there."

Miss Madden found the police as intimidating as what Dorothea used to call louts prowling round the cottage. For comfort she clutched Tilly's hand to prove to herself that she was flesh and blood, not a child-ghost who would at any moment float out of sight.

"I know." Tilly clapped her hands. "I'll go to the police station, report that a burglar is trying to break in, and they'll lie in wait and arrest him, put him in handcuffs and lock him in a cell."

Miss Madden began to tremble, remembering the policeman, no more than a boy, tampering with the windows and doors, questioning her until she grew muzzy-headed. Another one—or was he the same one?—telling her about a murder in the dark little wood. Violence, death, so terribly near. Right on her doorstep.

And now another bossy woman—there seemed to be an army of them—bent on forcing her to eat meals she didn't want, cleaning and sweeping, not replacing the furniture where it belonged, so that she would never know where to put her hand on anything. What had Dorothea preached to her? "Keep your troubles to yourself. Don't make a public exhibition of them." She swallowed twice, made an effort and found her voice. "Of course, it could be my fancy."

"Fancy!" Tilly wailed.

"Yes, my fancies, that's what my sister used to call them. 'You can't tell the difference between truth and the rigmarole of nonsense that goes round and round in your head.' Maybe I dreamed it," she whispered. "The wind. It could have been the wind, couldn't it, when it howls down the chimney?"

Tilly, cheated of drama and excitement, of being interrogated by the police, said crossly, "You mean you only imagined a man was trying to break into the house or steal the car? He wasn't there at all?"

Miss Madden locked her clenched hands one within the other. "The policeman would think I was a silly old woman. We won't bother him again." With Tilly beside her, the sun bright in the room, she willed herself to forget the threatening darkness of the night advancing towards her, the dread that squeezed her heart into a tight ball. "Suppose we have a clean up, make everything spick and span, show them I don't need any help."

Tilly sighed, accepted the anti-climax with ill-grace.

Miss Madden produced a raggy duster, which she flicked over odd surfaces, presented Tilly with a broom, with which she swept the crumbs under the rug. She picked the caramel off Miss Madden's slipper, decided it was inedible and set to washing up the crockery in cold water—there wasn't any hot.

At the end of ten minutes Miss Madden subsided into her chair, exhausted but triumphant. "Not a speck of dust to be seen. No need for them to come bothering me now."

Tilly thought it a slight exaggeration, but since dust was not offensive to her she made no comment. With an inadequate lunch behind her, she was becoming conscious of ravening hunger, with no hope of appeasing it now all the broken biscuits were eaten. Nothing for Miss Madden either.

"What will you have for supper?"

"A snack. Dorothea always said a heavy meal at night was bad for the digestion. Dinner at mid-day, and then a snack in the evening. That's what we always had. I shall drink some soup."

"Where is it?"

"In the kitchen. I think, but I can't be sure, it's in the cupboard above the sink."

One dented tin, the wrapper peeled off so that it could have contained anything. Tilly sawed at the lid with a blunt tin-opener, poured the contents into a saucepan. Tomato soup. Guiltily she sipped a couple of spoonfuls.

She went back to Miss Madden. "I've emptied it out of the tin, put it in a saucepan on the cooker, so you only have to warm it. You won't forget to drink it, will you?"

"I won't forget." Exhaustion was climbing upwards like a tide from Violet's ankles to her head. Hard as she tried to keep her eyes open, the lids kept drooping.

Tilly, feeling guilty at leaving Miss Madden hungry, which was a terrible thing to be, suddenly had a brain-wave. "I'll come and see you in the morning, and if Granny will lend me the money, I'll buy some fish and chips and run all the way, so they'll still be hot when I get here."

"Thank you, dear." For a second she couldn't remember who the dark-haired child was. Maybe she was part of a dream. Mercifully the fumes of bemusement were beginning to blot out loneliness and dread. She was far back in time, sedately pacing along the promenade with Dorothea, hypnotised by the gentle lace-frilled waves, her parents a few yards behind them.

"And don't forget to lock the door after me, and put the chain on. The back one is locked and all the window catches are fastened."

Violet nodded, smiled at the sea and sand, hearing Dorothea ordering her to pick up her feet and not dawdle. Yet when she woke in a dusk that was deepening into night, she was whimpering, her rheumatic leg so useless that she had to crawl up the stairs on all fours. Swamped with pain and desolation she forgot to lock the front door.

*

Nelia in a glow induced by three glasses of champagne—really, Bernard was too extravagant—beamed at Tilly. Safe! Well, of course, she was safe. She'd put all that silly, jittery nonsense behind her. "Did you see Miles? He was looking for you."

Impatiently, Tilly shook her head. "Granny, could I have my pocket money in advance this week? Please. It's terribly important."

Nelia with a slight feeling that her feet didn't quite touch the ground, that in some curious fashion she was air-borne—champagne always had this effect on her—tried to look scandalised. "What a little spendthrift you are! You know your grandfather doesn't approve of your having it in advance. However, I might, just for once." In her present state of mild euphoria, it was simpler to bend the rules than embroil herself in an exhausting battle of wills with Tilly.

*

Next morning, the 50p in her pocket, Tilly plotted a wide variety of subterfuges whereby she could elude Miles and by-pass her grandmother. All of which proved a wasted effort. Miles was closeted upstairs with his grandfather and *The Times* crossword, and her grandmother, after Tilly had wiped the breakfast dishes, made no protest when she walked out of the front door, through the gate.

Clutching one portion of cod and two portions of chips—the maximum available for 50p she arrived at the Tied Cottage to see a police car parked at the gate. So Miss Madden had told them about the burglar! Bursting with excitement, she ran, thrust open the front door and fell straight into the arms of Constable Rawlings, one of the two officers who had answered her S.O.S. from the telephone kiosk.

"Well, I never! Miss Sherlock Holmes in person!" He sniffed. "And what might you be doing distributing fish and chips at this time in the morning?"

Tilly's glance flew round the room. "Where's Miss Madden? Did the man get her?"

"Get her! What gave you that idea? What man?"

"The man who walked round and round the house all night, trying the windows and doors."

She heard the sound of footsteps, heavy ones, above her head. "Who's upstairs? Where's Miss Madden?"

"Sit down." The sardonic humour vanished. He eased her in a chair, sat directly opposite her. "Now what's all this about a man trying to break in? Who told you?"

"Miss Madden did. He frightened her. She thought he was going to strangle her, or steal her car. Why won't you tell me where she is?"

"I will. All in good time. First, suppose you tell me how long you've known Miss Madden."

"Ages. Weeks and weeks."

"And you visited her?" He sniffed again. "Brought her fish and chips?"

"She's my friend." More heavy footsteps overhead, sent her glance towards the ceiling. "Where is she?"

"She's in a nice, comfortable bed, being well looked after. She tripped and fell downstairs during the night, hurt herself a bit. That's why she had to be taken to hospital." He thought of the inert bundle of old clothes they'd loaded on to the ambulance. "Do your grandparents know you visit Miss Madden?"

"Of course they do."

He was startled to hear her choke on the words, surprised to discover that a child with a bent for sniffing out corpses was capable of normal human reactions. "No need for you to upset yourself. She's in good hands, with the doctors and nurses taking care of her." The meaningless phrases one automatically recited to next of kin. Except, it appeared, that Violet Madden, Spinster of this parish, possessed no kin. "Now, this man who walked round the house in the night, how often did Miss Madden complain about him?"

She slid him a sour look. "You made fun of me in the car, only pretended to believe there was a dead man, made a joke of it. But there was a dead man. I found him but you wouldn't let me go to the inquest."

He hung on to his patience. "You were of great assistance. I happen to know that the Chief Superintendent intends to write you a letter of appreciation for your quick thinking, the manner in which you reacted in an emergency. Meanwhile . . ."

"Have you arrested the murderer?"

He clenched his teeth, soldiered on. "Not yet." He opened the greaseproof bag, spread the contents before her. "Now suppose you eat your fish and chips and tell me exactly what Miss Madden said about a man prowling round the house."

"She could hear his footsteps." She thrust the greaseproof paper away. "They were for Miss Madden." Even so, she couldn't resist nibbling a chip. "But he couldn't break in because all the doors and windows were locked."

"I see." He kept the fact of the unlocked front door to himself.

"Sometimes Miss Madden thought there were two of them." Tilly caught sight of the fingerprinted powder splotched about the room, momentarily cheered up. "My prints!"

"Some of them may be."

"Will I have to come down to the police station?"

"We already have a set of yours on file, which means we can eliminate them. How did you come to meet Miss Madden?"

"In the supermarket. She'd dropped 50p and I found it and gave it to her. Then I carried her shopping bag home for her. And we had a super cake for tea."

"Are you quite sure that your grandparents know you were visiting Miss Madden, taking her food? That you weren't doing it off your own bat?"

"Of course I wasn't."

He checked her face: downbent, the lids shielding her eyes, mouth mutinous but wary. A lie. It didn't surprise him. All children, including his own, lied to ease themselves out of trouble. "How long has this prowler who frightened Miss Madden been walking round the house at night?"

Tilly shook her head, still not looking him in the eye. "I'm not sure. Mr. Pritchard might know. Why don't you ask him?"

"We've already questioned him. It was he who found Miss Madden unconscious at the bottom of the stairs and telephoned us. Tell me the last time you saw her?"

"Yesterday. In the afternoon. A horrid bossy woman was here trying to make her have a Home Help and Meals on Wheels which she didn't want. It made her cry, so after she'd gone, we cleaned up and I left her some soup. Did she drink it?"

"No."

"I wish she had. She must have been terribly hungry. There was nothing to eat for tea."

"Did she talk to you about herself?"

"Sometimes about her sister who's dead. She was called Dorothea. And Sammy, he was her cat, and he was run over."

"Yes, I've heard about him. Where was she when you left her yesterday afternoon?"

"Sitting in the chair you're sitting in."

"All right, was she? Talked to you, did she?"

"Of course. We always talked."

He snapped his note-book shut, encircled it in a rubber band. "Now you sit there and eat your fish and chips and as soon as the two officers have finished upstairs, I'll give you a lift home."

The odours of sodden, greasy paper, congealing chips and cold fish nauseated Tilly. The lovely warm picture of spreading her gift of food under Miss Madden's nose, splitting the fish into two portions, counting out the chips into two equal piles was destroyed. Realism exploded into grief and bewilderment. She stared at Constable Rawlings, hating his condescending smile, his feigned indulgence, felt the sting of tears on her eyeballs and with a turn of speed that caught Rawlings unawares launched into flight.

"Hi, come back," he shouted, but she was beyond earshot.

Detective Inspector Warren appeared on the landing, shouted, "What's going on?"

"The kid. Old Colonel Furston's granddaughter. At it again! Born with a natural bent for hogging the limelight. Apparently she knew the old lady, brought her food. Swore the old girl was terrified of a man, or men, who prowled round the house at night. True or false, your guess is as good as mine."

"Let her go, did you?"

"She made off. But we know where to find her."

"No footprints, inside or out. Not that there are likely to be any on the brick paths in this weather. But you and Bates better do a second check. The carpet on the third stair from the top is frayed down to the canvas, and one slipper is lying halfway down. She could have caught her toe in it, fallen headlong. Or she could have been pushed. Either way, she came out of it with a fractured skull."

*

Deacon glanced up from the report on Miss Madden, thankful that a missing child the other side of the county had drawn off about two thirds of the men who had been drafted in to cover the Rampton murder. With the exception of a few miscalled "experts," he was back to his small tight squad. Which suited him. Excruciatingly polite young officers still wet behind the ears, stuck in his gorge.

"Anything stolen?" he demanded. "Drawers opened, cupboards ransacked?"

"No, sir. No sign of disturbance."

"The cat woman, I understand?"

"That's right, sir."

"How did the Furston kid come to get involved with the old lady?"

"They met in a supermarket. The child picked up a 50p the old lady had dropped. Apparently she used to look in and see her. Doesn't remember how often."

"With her grandparents' permission?"

"Says so, but I'd be inclined to doubt it. A lone ranger, that one."

"And no fingerprints except those of the child, Miss Madden, Pritchard, and the woman from the Social Services?"

"That's so, sir."

"This man Pritchard. A likely suspect—always supposing there was any foul play?"

"Wouldn't think so, but we'll still investigate him. He was pretty cut up about the old girl. He found her. Confirms the child's story about Miss Madden believing she heard a prowler, or more than one, trying to break in. The front door was unlocked, so that anyone could have walked in."

"Anything worth stealing?"

"There was a cash-box upstairs with £99.50 in it. Hadn't been touched. Also five pounds and some silver in the kitchen drawer. Odd bits of jewellery of no value: a watch, and a wedding ring that had probably been her mother's. The car Pritchard says she was forever fretting about, still locked in the garage. Until she comes to, sir, we aren't able to confirm whether or not anything was taken."

"What's the latest bulletin?"

"Dicey, could go either way."

"Have another go at Pritchard. Neighbours interrogated, I take it?"

"So far as there are any. The cottage is pretty isolated. It's no more than a couple of hundred yards from where Rampton was murdered."

"We're all aware of that! It doesn't seem to have got us anywhere. And if you're still hooked on the idea of tracking down a car with blood on the bumper and a number-plate ending with 4, forget it. Remember the cat was dead and buried a week before Rampton was murdered—unless Pritchard is lying his head off."

W.P.C. Edwards tapped on the door, opened it. "Mr. Masters is here, sir. He says he has an appointment with you."

"Show him in." He looked up at Warren. "Keep at it. I'd like another report by 5:30. And for God's sake, steer clear of that child. Colonel Furston has a very low boiling point. I don't fancy another hassle with him."

Deacon half rose, stretched out a hand. "Ah, Mr. Masters, you wanted to see me." His memory retained only a vague outline of Arnold Masters who, to the best of his belief, he had only met once at his mother's house when the old lady had summoned him, ordered him forthwith to arrest and imprison the vandals who had robbed her apple orchard. A regular old tartar! It must be four years, maybe a bit more, since the Manor House had been sold, and Lady Masters had been moved to a flat in London, where she had died a few months later.

Since Arnold Masters no longer owned any property in the neighbourhood, he couldn't imagine why he'd been at pains to make an appointment with him. The sum of Deacon's knowledge of the man was that he was some breed of financier, a wheeler and dealer, who'd never done an honest day's work in his life. But looks hadn't come his way. He was a good two stone overweight—not that Deacon could talk—with small, what Deacon called sliding eyes, jutting brows, skin polished with rich living, a thrusting aggressive manner.

"So what can I do for you, Mr. Masters?"

"The boot's on the other foot. I'm here to do you a good turn."

"Indeed!"

"As you are probably aware, after my mother's death, I moved to South Africa. The Cape. It's a good life out there, especially for kids." Always provided, Deacon added silently, their skin was the acceptable colour. "I should explain that my mother was a compulsive hoarder. A human squirrel. She never threw away a bill, a scrap of paper, kept diaries going back to the end of the last century, which she stored in heavy-duty leather trunks. There were twenty of them, each weighing over half a hundredweight."

He paused for Deacon's response, and when none was forthcoming, continued, "I had them shipped out to the Cape, stored in an attic. I was tempted to make a bonfire of the lot, then realised I had the family to consider . . . our personal history covering over half a century." He glanced at Deacon, expectant of interest, a nod of approval, received neither. "Then two months ago I came a cropper on a horse, was laid up and while I was on my back I occupied myself sorting and sifting. Fortunately I started on the later boxes, worked backwards."

Deacon allowed himself a meaningful glance at his watch. It had no effect on Masters. "You'll remember that the Manor was sold in the spring of 1974 when my mother's health was steadily deteriorating and it became advisable for her to move to London, be under the care of a London specialist. There was also a staffing problem. Eleven bedrooms! A maze of them, and all for one old lady!"

Deacon murmured, "I don't see . . ."

"I know you don't, but you will. An eighteenth-century manor house on twenty acres of grounds is a valuable, much-sought-after property. Rampton's, who were handling the sale, put a reserve price on it of one hundred thousand pounds."

"Indeed!"

The irony sent a rush of blood to Masters' bulging cheeks. "I'll come to the point, Superintendent. A week before the auction my mother saw fit to sell the Manor House to the Nugents for fifty thousand pounds, half the reserve price. A private deal."

Deacon stared at him. Masters was obviously cherishing a grudge at being tricked out of a sizable portion of his inheritance. So what action was he supposed to take? "Since the property belonged to your mother, presumably she was at liberty to sell it to whom she chose. Privately or otherwise. I take it, it wasn't entailed?"

"No, it wasn't. But as her only child, I had a right to assume that, in due course, the proceeds of the sale would revert to me, or to my children. Instead she cheated me out of fifty thousand pounds!"

"I'm afraid I don't follow you, Mr. Masters." This time he glanced openly at his watch. "And I'm afraid I'm running short of time."

Masters' natural arrogance exploded. "I suggest you make a little more. It will be to your advantage. The only soft spot in my mother's make-up was for kids. The Nugents, the present owners of Fernwell Manor, have five. Rose Nugent had always been a pet of my mother's, and she was sentimentally attached to all Rose's children, but particularly to the eldest boy, Nicholas. It's my guess that Rose and her husband were guilty of exerting undue influence on an aged invalid to persuade her to sell them the Manor at a price half its market value. They succeeded. Ten days before the auction, privately, without a whisper to anyone, she sold them the Manor. She also negotiated a very favourable mortgage they still haven't paid off. An undercover operation, one for which she needed an accomplice. And I've got evidence to prove it. Here . . ." He tugged a small leather-bound book out of his pocket. "Read it for yourself. My mother's diary. April 30th."

Deacon accepted the offering. Crabbed writing, in places smudged. He skimmed through the takings at a church bazaar, the sacking of an under-gardener, a last item of three sentences. "Rose to tea. Calmed her fears. Assured her all would go through without a hitch provided she held her tongue."

Bored, Deacon suggested, "Your mother obviously negotiated the sale of the Manor House without consulting you. No law against it. Not a criminal offence. Hardly a matter for the police."

"No. If you'll refer to May 14th, the first line, you may change your mind. Any right-thinking man would."

Deacon read it. "To one crook £5,000."

"A bribe," Masters snarled, leaning forward, almost spitting the words in Deacon's face. "My mother bribed someone in Rampton's employ to oil the wheels, look the other way, not spill the beans, speed up the sale so that it would be finalised before the auction date. As she wrote in her own hand, a cheat and a crook who lined his pockets. Bit of an actor too, in that he would have had to appear stunned when he learned the property had been sold behind Rampton's back, the agreement broken."

"You're accusing a member of Rampton's staff of acting unethically, robbing the firm who employed him, pocketing a bribe?"

"You bet I am." The smirk was openly contemptuous. "And now Rampton's dead. Makes you think, doesn't it?"

"Ah," Deacon breathed. "You're suggesting that there is a link between Rampton's murder and your mother's disposal of her property?"

"Right the first time. Someone made himself a nice little nest-egg out of a crooked deal. Stands out a mile. And I was the loser, twice over. Once on a sale that was fiddled and secondly by some scoundrel who blackmailed my mother out of £5,000."

Deacon tapped the diary. "When you found this among your mother's papers, you flew to London?"

"As soon as I was fit to travel." He squared his shoulders. "I happen to be old-fashioned, to believe in justice."

Not only pomposity but platitudes! "What action did you take?"

"I telephoned Rampton, put him wise."

"On what date?"

"August 6th. Around 4 P.M."

"The afternoon of the night Rampton was murdered?"

"Yes."

"How did Rampton react when you spoke to him?"

"He promised to look into it."

"Today's the 27th. Rampton's murder received wide coverage in the local and national press. It didn't occur to you to contact us earlier?"

"Circumstances prevented it. My wife collapsed that evening, was admitted as an emergency into the London Clinic. Tumour. Proved to be non-malignant, but there were complications and for quite a while it was touch and go."

"I'm sorry. I hope she is making a good recovery."

"Yes."

"Even so, presumably at some time during that period of anxiety you picked up a newspaper, learned that Rampton had been murdered?"

"I did. I was interested to learn who you'd arrested. And since no arrest had been made, as soon as my wife was off the danger list, I telephoned you to make this appointment. It seemed to me you could do with a little help."

"Good of you," Deacon murmured perfunctorily. He welcomed it as a promising lead, but he couldn't bring himself to express gratitude to a man whose avarice and vindictiveness were as palpable as a taint in the air. "Naturally, we'd like a full statement from you. I'll have someone take it down."

When no gratitude, even thanks were forthcoming, Masters thrust out his jaw. "Rampton would never have stood for a crooked deal. Any employee of his who'd been a party to a sale that broke an agreement made in good faith and robbed him of his commission, would have been fired on the spot. I've provided you with information that should enable you to bring the murderer to justice." With eyes made small by venom and the cushions of fat on his cheeks, he demanded, "What action do you propose to take?"

"Immediate action. I agree that both Rampton and his father were honourable men." A quality to which Masters had no claim . . . a man obsessed with pursuing a vendetta beyond the grave against his mother. It happened that Deacon had a sentimental attachment to all mothers. An only child, his own had been widowed when he was eight years old. His memory of the evening of the funeral was as vivid as if it had been yesterday. When all the mourners had drifted away, they had sat on either side of the kitchen grate. "Now there's only you and me, Arthur. The last thing your dad would have wanted was for us to sit around moping. And we won't. We're going to make him proud of us. You working hard at school, making something of yourself, and me, well, there's lots of jobs I can turn my hand to. Already Mr. Barnes has offered me an afternoon job behind his counter. And evening there's dressmaking. Be a credit to him, that's our aim in life."

And she'd succeeded, lived to reach her 84th birthday a year ago. He still missed her, that limitless, enduring love that never faltered, her abiding faith that took it for granted he could move mountains. Mothers to him were sacrosanct.

"I wonder if I might ask you a personal question, Mr. Masters. Your mother was a wealthy woman. Who were her main beneficiaries?"

"She made various bequests to a wide range of charities, most of them concerned with animal welfare. The remainder was divided into seven equal Trust Funds for my son and daughter and the five Nugent children, to mature when each reached the age of twenty-one."

Though he spoke tersely, without raising his voice, there was an undertone of remorseless hate which would endure as long as he lived. He had, to use a cliché, been robbed.

When the detective-sergeant who had been summoned to take down Masters' statement knocked on the door, Deacon rose, opened it, but omitted to shake Masters' hand.

When he was alone, Deacon sifted through the statements

on his desk, extracted one that had been typed by P.C. Strawson—apparently with one finger and two thumbs. Inspector Warren's briefing to Strawson and his co-driver, Allen, had been to make a reccy of No. 12 Lane End, a house owned and occupied by Edmund Lang. They'd examined it from a distance, observed by peering through two panes of glass set high in the garage that there was no car, proceeded to the rear, to discover the back door was ajar. When there was no response to their knocks, they'd embarked on an inspection of the interior. Well maintained, exceptionally tidy. Nothing to arouse suspicion. They had also walked round the garden, taken note of the well.

In Deacon's estimation they'd been guilty of exceeding their duty. He'd told Warren as much, rapped his knuckles. While Lang hadn't been cleared, no evidence had yet been produced to warrant the entry of his house without possession of a search warrant.

Having read the statement twice, Deacon returned it to its file. Ten, even five years ago, householders blithely left their doors unlocked. But not now, when petty thieves could be skulking behind any patch of cover, prepared to snatch a purse, odd pieces of silver, even clothing, then disappear into thin air.

Absent-mindedness? Could be. Though Lang's manner, cool, astute, unwasteful of words, had not suggested he'd be subject to lapses of memory. Equally, it could have been a gesture of bravado. Not a man to make inspired guesses, snap judgments, the cogs on his brain began to tick over slowly, as he masticated his thoughts, taking his time, confiding in nobody.

TEN

Surprise lent Rose Nugent's voice a breathlessness. "Superintendent Deacon? Yes, of course, if he wishes to see me. Do you know why?"

W.P.C. Edwards said no, enquired if it would be convenient for the Superintendent to call at five o'clock.

"We're having a young people's tennis party. It's all a bit disorganised. As long as the Superintendent doesn't object to a gang of youngsters around the place."

W.P.C. Edwards said she was sure he wouldn't and putting the phone down, raised her eyes to the ceiling. "Anyone for tennis!" she mimicked. "I thought that went out with the first world war."

"Gracious living!" The young police cadet winked. "Not your scene, baby."

The pit-pat of balls, an umpire calling the score was audible behind a screen of shrubs. As the constable opened the car door, Rose Nugent appeared at the top of a curving flight of stone steps. A delicately-boned, wandlike blonde, she fitted to perfection the rôle of châtelaine of a seventeenth-century manor house. Her hand in Deacon's was so fragile he took care to exert the minimum of pressure. "I've disturbed you; I apologise."

"No, no." The smile was serenely forbearing. "They've all been fed, and shouldn't be calling for iced drinks for another hour. I thought we'd go into my husband's study. It's sheltered. By that I mean no balls are likely to bounce against the window, and my two youngest won't make hobgoblin faces at us. They're twins. At that ghastly inquisitive age."

A man's room, sombre, the predominating colours rust and brown. Deacon subsided into a handsome studded leather armchair that he'd have been glad to claim as his own: with the seat exactly the right height from the ground. "You'll be wondering why I'm here. Bothering you!"

"And hoping you're going to put me out of my suspense."

"I'd like to talk to you about Lady Masters. How well did you know her?"

She moistened her lips, focused her gaze slightly to his right, her voice low pitched but assured. "The best way I can describe her is that she was the grandmother figure in my life. I had no grandparents of my own; they died before I was born. My mother . . . well, she was a compulsive traveller; in her natural element in empty spaces, sleeping under the stars, preferably in some desert, surrounded by camels! She died when I was eighteen. My father was a member of Parliament, extremely conscientious with a constituency in the North of England which took him away from home for long periods. To me he was a kind but remote figure. That is probably why, when I was growing up, Lady Masters played a key rôle in my life, a sort of centre-piece." A pale rose flush tinted the translucent skin. "Also we were both fundamentally lonely, and lonely people recognise one another on sight." Suddenly her eyes shimmered, radiance bloomed. "She introduced me to Tim, my husband, magicked him from somewhere because she knew by instinct . . . well, that we'd be perfect for each other. As we are." She made a gesture with her hands. "She gave me my husband, my children. I loved her. It was as simple as that."

Deacon, assuming his most avuncular pose smiled. A spontaneous tribute, or one rehearsed and tucked away for use in an emergency? Innocent, or guilty? No telling . . . yet. "And she, by all accounts, loved you?"

"I like to think she did. It's so important to be loved when you're young."

"Yet not everyone accounted her a likeable woman, did they?"

"No. She could be arrogant, sometimes even cruel, and she

held tight to her grudges. Above all, latterly, she bitterly resented that her life was, inevitably, coming to its end. She was jealous of the people who would be alive when she was dead."

"When you're dead you're dispossessed of power over the living. They're free."

The radiance in her face switched itself off. "Superintendent, would you be good enough to explain why you are here?"

"Yes, of course. But first there are one or two questions I'd like answered." Without waiting for her permission, he went on, "She and her only child, Arnold Masters, didn't, so I'm given to understand, enjoy the happiest of relationships."

"That was so."

"Why was that?"

"They had nothing in common. Latterly she believed, rightly or wrongly, he was sitting around waiting for her to die."

"When it became impracticable for her to maintain this house, she sold it to you and your husband?"

"Yes." The single word, edged with hauteur, rebuked his impertinence.

"Though there were other potential buyers who would have paid a considerably higher price for the property?"

He'd succeeded in his aim, triggered off a flash of anger. "Is that your business, Superintendent?"

"I'm afraid it is." He put on his most avuncular smile. "Lady Masters had been a willing party to an agreement with Rampton whereby the Manor House was to be auctioned to the highest bidder. A signed agreement she broke without advising either her son or the auctioneers she had no intention of honouring it."

"The house belonged to her. She had a right to sell it to whom she chose."

"Granted. No crime. All she could be accused of was discourtesy, unethical behaviour. Shall we say conduct unbecoming to a gentlewoman."

"That's your view, Superintendent, not mine."

"What I find mystifying is why she agreed to a public auction if, as transpired, she had already decided to sell the Manor House to you and your husband."

"She had her reasons, and they are of no concern to anyone else." She hesitated, then added reluctantly, "Also, she had suffered a minor stroke." For the first time exasperation broke in her. "Really, Superintendent, I can't see the purpose of this interrogation."

"I'm sorry if you regard it as such. I have no intention of embarrassing you. Now, I would be grateful if you would describe the course of Lady Masters' illness. Was it a severe stroke?"

"No, comparatively minor, but for several weeks, it affected her speech and her right hand. This made it difficult for her to communicate." She moistened her lips, stared straight ahead of her, avoiding Deacon's glance. "Arnold was quick to take advantage of his mother's weakness. He persuaded . . . if that is the word . . . her into signing the agreement with Rampton's, hoping she would forget she had put her signature to the document. Later, when she had partially recovered, she swore that he had guided the pen. Whether or not that was true, I don't know. She could have imagined it."

"She made a complete recovery?"

"Not complete, but her speech became near-normal, and she could write, though slowly, with great effort. And if you're proposing to ask me, as I'm sure you are, whether she was mentally affected, in any way senile, the answer is no. She was as keen-witted, as clear-headed as she'd always been."

"Good. What happened next?"

She watched two children race by the window, then turned an accusing gaze on him. "You'll misunderstand. Without knowing either me or my husband, you can't fail to. It's not . . ."

He guessed she'd only just bitten back the spoilt child's perennial complaint. It's not fair. "Try me."

"Arnold had always actively resented that his mother cared more for our children than his own. He believed, quite wrongly, that Tim and I influenced his mother. That wasn't so. She took advice from no one." She finished with muted rage,

"Oh, it sounds so ugly, as though Tim and I took advantage of her affection for us and the children. We didn't."

"No, I'm sure you didn't. How was the deal finalised?"

"Very simply between our solicitor and hers. They both drove down from London for the signing of the deeds, brought their clerks with them to act as witnesses."

"No one else was involved?"

"No."

"Not even in a minor rôle? You're certain?"

"I'm not a liar, Superintendent."

"No, of course not. Where did Lady Masters keep the deeds of the Manor House?"

"In London, with her solicitor."

Deacon leaned forward. "Mrs. Nugent, you're a young woman, that means that your memory is sharp. Can you assure me that there was no one other than you, your husband, two legal advisers and Lady Masters who was aware she intended without informing her son to sell the Manor to you at half the reserve price it was likely to have fetched at a public auction?"

"Yes." She paused, lowered her eyes to hide her resentment at his interrogation, then shrugged pettishly. "Perhaps I should explain, otherwise you'll jump to a wrong conclusion. My husband was extremely upset at the manner in which the sale was conducted, that he might be counted guilty of having behaved dishonourably. The afternoon before the solicitors were due to arrive, he begged, yes begged, Lady Masters to reconsider her decision, allow the auction to go ahead, and told her that we'd take our chance. And although there wasn't a hope we could buy the Manor at the reserve price, he meant what he said. Lady Masters refused to listen to him, became so distraught that we were both afraid she might bring on another stroke. She insisted that she'd been tricked into signing the agreement with Rampton's. That such a sale could not be enforced in law; and that there was no means by which Arnold could attack the validity of the sale." She concluded on a haughty, slightly derisive note. "To put your mind at rest, Superintendent, I swear that neither my husband nor I exerted any pressure on her."

"And when the news of the private sale became public, what was Arnold Masters' reaction?"

"My children would describe it as 'blowing his top.' He literally foamed at the mouth, threatened to have doctors brought down from London to have his mother declared to be of unsound mind. She laughed, told him to go ahead and waste his money. I've no idea whether or not he made any attempt to have her certified."

"And Mr. Rampton?"

"He never contacted us, but I know he called to see Lady Masters and demanded to know why she had broken her agreement with them, involved them in pre-sale expenses which they had no way of recouping. Whether or not he sent her a bill, and if so whether she paid it, I wouldn't know."

Voices sounded in the hall. She rose to her feet, refrained from looking directly at him. "That's all I can tell you, Superintendent. If you wish, you can discuss the matter with my husband, though he won't be home until eight."

Deacon rose. "I won't trouble him. If I need to get in touch with him, I'll telephone."

Though she didn't offer it, he took the fragile, lifeless hand. "Thank you, I'll see myself out."

Though he felt no pity for her, was of the opinion that she'd bent the truth to fulfil a life-time's ambition, and on the way stoked a few fires of discord, he had a measure of admiration for her cool diplomacy over the years. Rose Nugent was more than a pretty face.

Back at the station, Deacon ordered the desk clerk to summon Warren. In theory, particularly on a murder case, the Fernwell station operated as a force. In practice, Deacon sealed off areas for himself, delighting in producing cats out of bags.

"I want," he said before Warren had closed the door, "a list of the employees at Rampton's three offices. Names, ages, the dates when they joined the firm. Any that left three or four years ago. And quick."

To jog a memory that appeared to be deteriorating, Warren said, "We already have detailed statements on all of them."

"Not detailed enough," Deacon retorted. "I want a report on their hobbies, life-style, the figures on their monthly pay cheques."

"It's half past six. All three offices are closed. Do you wish me to interview the managers at home?"

"Yes." Deacon stared into space, mouth pursed, brow lowering, no longer anyone's favourite uncle. As Warren reached the door, he abruptly changed his mind. "On second thoughts, leave Lang until the morning. Thanks to Strawson and Allen tramping round the place, he's probably aware they turned it over, has got all his answers prepared. Proof that he's as pure as the driven snow! How's the old lady whose cat was run over?"

"Still in a coma."

Warren, to emphasise that they were instantly available, collected three files, placed them on Deacon's desk. They were received without comment.

Alone, Deacon to refresh his memory flipped through them again.

Three offices, three managers, none of whom, to outward appearances, had appreciably raised their living standards during the last four years in that their addresses hadn't changed. Simons, at Fernwell, lived in an oasthouse he'd converted when he'd been married six years ago. A year later Reynolds, when his wife developed arthritis, had moved to a bungalow that must have cost him a packet, except his wife, a comparatively wealthy woman, had probably paid for it. Lang, a bachelor, occupied the cottage he'd moved into when he was taken on the Anderbridge pay-roll. Junior members of the staff made do with flats or lived at home with parents. Salaries had barely kept up with inflation. Nothing he hadn't known weeks ago.

He chose to walk home in that exercise sometimes stimulated and clarified his thought processes. A third of the way there, on the outskirts of the town, his glance travelled across the street, focused on a silhouette behind a window on the first floor of the local branch of a Building Society. No prize for guessing whose it was. Andrew Scott, a glutton for work, was sitting martyrlike at his desk. What, Deacon asked himself, not for the first time, was the average man's biggest investment in a life-time? His house. And how many men were in a position to buy their houses outright? Only those who owned a property of equal value or were at the receiving end of a substantial hand-out.

He had to wait before Scott, face soured by being disturbed out of office hours appeared. Deacon lifted a placating hand. "I know, I know! You're just leaving, but it's a simple enquiry. Won't keep you more than a minute."

"I'm on the point of locking up, going home." As evidence Scott clasped his bowler hat to his chest.

"I have to ask you for some confidential information."

"Quite out of the question."

"Three names. Leonard Simons. James Reynolds. Edmund Lang."

"What about them?"

"Customers of yours?"

"Really, Superintendent!"

"I know, I know, you're not allowed to divulge customers' names. Unethical." He lowered his voice. "I could, of course, obtain a warrant, but that would further delay your arrival home."

Andrew Scott, cornered, glowered. "Simons and Reynolds yes. That is all the information I can reveal."

"Not Lang?"

To side-step a verbal lie, Scott gave the merest shake of his head.

"Has he ever been a customer of yours?"

"Superintendent, that is all the confidential information I am prepared to divulge. If you require more, I suggest you produce that warrant."

"Fair enough. Thanks." Deacon found himself facing a locked door behind which Scott had retreated.

*

For Anna, time was suspended in a vacuum. She lay like an effigy on the rumpled bed, mourning the loss of the precious voice; racked by guilt that she had failed him, was destined forever to exist in an abyss of loneliness. In an effort to coax the voice back to life she muffled all extraneous sound by holding the palms of her hands over her ears. Silence except for the measured throb of a metronome in her temples.

The telephone beside the bed rang three times before, with a hand that was as heavy as if it were weighted with lead, she lifted the hand-set.

"Oh, Anna, you are home! I've been trying to reach you, and couldn't. I was worried . . ." Anthea's normal insipid voice teetered on the verge of hysteria. "Usually when you work at home, you let me know ahead, but you didn't say a word last evening. You're not ill, are you?"

Anna's voice clotted in her throat, blurring her consonants. "Headache. Took some dope. Okay tomorrow."

As exhausted as though she'd completed some Herculean task, she dropped the phone, lay back on the pillows, drowsed. Waking hours later consciousness drove a spike through her heart. Why, why had he rejected her? Because she'd been unable to convince that fat fool of a policeman that Carol and lover-boy had murdered Garth? Because she'd failed to retrieve his father's watch from a child thief? Because he knew, as she did, that Edmund was lying? Hiding something. Doing a cover-up. She'd sensed the lies the moment he'd stumbled into the sitting-room to blurt out that Garth was dead. But, literally pole-axed by shock, been unable to pin down why he should lie. Now, as though attacked from the rear, she was struck by a suspicion so monstrous that her flesh shivered on her bones: that Edmund knew, had known all the time that those two degenerate, money-hungry kids had murdered Garth, danced round his grave. Why else should he try to persuade her they were innocent? She saw them both caught in the act, swearing him to secrecy, promising to pay him hush-money when they grabbed their fortune. Like any deprived child, Edmund was greedy for money. Her child!

She hauled herself up on her right arm, swung herself to the edge of the bed. Her left arm and leg were numb, the result, she told herself, of an awkward posture during the night.

Upright, her head swam, became incapable of coherent thought. What time was it? What day? She peered at the clock face. A quarter to four. She snapped off the light. A three-quarter moon spun a gauze of light over the room. For a while she swayed rhythmically on the edge of the bed. Tuesday? Wednesday? A tiresome jigsaw not worth struggling to solve. Thirst had parched her throat to the texture of sandpaper. Taking one step at a time, fumbling for the light switches, she descended to the hall, crouched on the bottom stair until she'd regained sufficient strength to haul herself upright, plot a path to the drinks cupboard. Half the whisky she poured ran down her nightdress. Sprawled in the arm-chair she drank the rest neat. A minute later, the glass slipped to the floor and she was asleep.

Uncountable hours later she surfaced centimetre by centimetre into consciousness like one emerging from the bowels of the earth. When the long haul was completed she was riven by an appalling sense of aloneness: of being severed from human kind. Yet it was a stoical acceptance of her isolation that steeled her determination to catechise Edmund. Squeeze the truth out of Baby Carol and lover-boy. Mechanically massaging the weighted hand, what she must set herself to do presented itself in a series of still-life pictures.

She brooded for an hour and then when the clock on the mantel chimed nine times, she hoisted herself to her feet, took the stairs one at a time like a child learning to walk, contemplated a bath, renounced it and turned on the shower. It was not until she was sitting on her dressing-stool that the dripping tails of hair provided evidence that unknowingly she'd allowed the water to swirl over her head. With her left hand too much of an effort to lift until the circulation revived, she mopped up most of the cascading water with her right. It took her an hour to dress because her clothes infuriatingly played tricks on her, one moment in her hand, the next on the floor.

Upright, she looked in the long mirror, stared at a stranger.

She blinked, shook her head to clear her vision, but the stranger was still there. When she lifted her hand to sweep back the lank soaked hair, the stranger mocked her by repeating the gesture. She screamed an obscenity at her, then lurched out of mirror's reach.

The car had been parked all night in the drive, a lapse for which Garth would have scolded her. With an effort she manoeuvred herself into the driving seat, switched on the ignition, reversed and found herself careering across the circular lawn, stamped on the brake and narrowly missed colliding with one of the gate pillars.

She cursed the numb left hand that obstinately refused to obey her then managed to hook it through the spoke of the steering wheel which gave her some leverage. Since the car was automatic the semi-immobility of her left leg didn't matter. The numbness, she promised herself, would soon be replaced by spasms of pins and needles as the blood began to circulate.

After three crawling miles via roads that circled the town she braked, grinned derision at the house she counted an eyesore on the landscape: outflung wings on different levels, ostentatious, flaunting its vulgarity, an excrescence dreamed up by the *nouveau riche* of which Baby Carol was assuredly a founder member. How Garth must have loathed it! She abandoned the car in the middle of the road, walked up the drive at a pace made uneven by the dragging foot.

She rang the bell. When no one answered she pressed her face against the nearest window. Curtained in pleated net. She rang the bell a second time, holding her finger rigid on it for a quarter of a minute. A voice called over a planting of conifers, "You won't find anyone in."

A stumpy middle-aged woman with grey hair fitting close to her head in lacquered undulations, eyed her with haughty disapproval, repeated, "There's no one at home."

"Where are they?"

The pale blue myopic gaze of the woman on the far side of the hedge examined the caller's ill-assorted garments, puffy, dough-coloured face, splashed with flames of scarlet on the cheekbones, drew back. "I told you, there's no one at home."

Anna advanced on the hedge. "I want their address."

"I don't have it."

"Liar," Anna screeched a second before she became conscious of a choking sensation in her throat, a sudden cloudiness of vision. She fought her way to what she believed was clarity. "They murdered my husband. My brother was a witness to . . ." But her vocal cords had ceased to function, striking her dumb, her mouth reduced to a hole in her face.

The woman retreated, recoiling from a sight that revolted her, calling, "Neil . . . Neil . . ."

A middle-aged, stoutish man materialised at her side. "Yes, dear."

She said nothing, left him to draw his own conclusions. He wound a protective arm round his wife's shoulders. "Sorry we can't help. If you're in trouble, I suggest you contact the police." With a quick, firm step he guided his wife to the front door, closed it behind them. His wife settled in a chair, he parted the curtains. "My God, she's driving, and on the wrong side of the road. I'll telephone the police. She's a menace to oncoming traffic."

The woman over-ruled him. "We don't want to get involved, dear. She's quite obviously drunk. Don't worry, she'll be picked up by the first patrol car that spots her." She smiled relief at having disposed of an embarrassing situation. "I know it's early, but I think a small brandy would do us both good, don't you?"

"Perhaps you're right, dear."

*

In the corner of the drawing-room was a small *écritoire* inlaid with swirling tendrils and exotic foliage at which Nelia sat to write her letters, tot up the tradesmen's bills. Tilly stood over it mesmerised by the pile of small change: her heart's desire within reach of her hand! The coins were clasped in her fist when Nelia gasped, "Tilly!" causing three parts of them to cascade over the floor.

Nelia's mouth gaped in horror. "Tilly, how could you? Stealing money. I actually saw you. Stealing!"

"For my bus fare because I've spent all my pocket money on fish and chips for Miss Madden and now she's ill in hospital and I have to go and see her."

Nelia struggled to establish one basic fact. "Who is Miss Madden?"

"My friend."

"Where does she live?"

"On the road near the wood." A near hysterical Tilly, pleaded, "Oh, please, please, lend me some money for my bus fare." There followed an incoherent frenzied stream of words which were gibberish in Nelia's ears. Miss Madden dropping her change, Tilly picking it up, returning it to her; a cat that had been run over; some man called Pritchard who owned a dog; Tilly cleaning a house, a tin of soup; police who'd found Miss Madden injured at the foot of the stairs. She didn't believe a word of it. If Tilly was capable of stealing money, it followed that she was guilty of spinning a string of lies to worm herself out of trouble. She closed her eyes as though to screen herself from the ugly sordidness of deceit, then immediately opened them again. "The police! You mean they're coming here again?"

"No," Tilly said dolefully. "They don't have to because they've got my fingerprints on record."

Though it was an impossible feat, Nelia supposed she should be grateful for the smallest mercy. Behind her lay a night in which Reggie had been restless, in pain, her sleep reduced to three hours. As though the ceiling above her head was transparent she could see Reggie toiling to dress himself, an exhausting process that left him irascible for hours, coming downstairs step by step to learn that his granddaughter was a thief. She shook a threatening finger in Tilly's face. "I forbid you to repeat a word of this to your grandfather. Is that understood?"

"Yes." Tilly sighed, pleaded. "But I'm her friend. She'd want me to go and see her in hospital, I know she would."

Tilly, as usual maddeningly side-tracking the main issue.

"Children are not allowed to visit patients in hospital unless in the company of an adult. This woman? You've never once mentioned her. Are you making her up? Is she one of your fairy stories?" Not a man in a dirty rain-coat, but a woman, sly, malodorous, preying on a child! "I want the truth."

Tilly wailed, "She was hungry and now she's hurt herself. She's old with nothing to eat, that's why I promised her the fish and chips. I must go and see her or she'll think I've broken my promise."

Nelia reverted to the belief that Tilly was spinning a web of lies. There was no old lady, only, with the stolen change in her pocket, the prospect of a bus ride for Tilly. "Miss Madden? Are you certain that was her name?"

"Miss Violet Madden."

Nelia, desperate to have the non-existence of Miss Madden disposed of before Reggie began, with immense effort, to descend the stairs, clinched the deal. "Very well, I'll telephone the hospital and enquire how she is."

Nelia looked up the number, dialled, watching Tilly for signs of guilt or apprehension, finding none. There was a lengthy interval before she was connected with the right ward. "Thank you," she breathed. Miss Madden existed, was occupying a bed in Ward 6 of Fernwell General Hospital.

"Why do you have to be so secretive, to go visiting old ladies on the sly?"

Tilly's voice was a hoarse whisper. "How is she?"

"Comfortable." Nelia lied as she pocketed the tainted money. "If I hadn't caught you in the act, you'd have stolen the money, wouldn't you?"

"For my bus fare. Only for my bus fare."

The thump of Reggie's crutches sounded on the landing overhead, and Nelia hurried towards the door, fiercely whispering, "Remember, not a word to your grandfather."

During the morning she kept Tilly covered under a rota system. "I'm sure I don't know why you fuss," Mrs. Baker complained after being told for the third time to locate Tilly.

"She's safe enough, up in her bedroom, writing to that dog of hers."

At the first opportunity Nelia drew Miles aside. "Miles dear, have you ever heard Tilly talk about a Miss Madden?"

Baffled, he shook his head. "No, Granny."

She sighed. "It seems that Tilly has been visiting an old lady who isn't known to us. It's very worrying. Now the old lady, at least I think she's old, has been taken to hospital after a fall and Tilly is begging to be allowed to visit her. That, of course, is quite out of the question. Young children without an adult aren't allowed into hospital wards. Your grandfather would be most upset if he learnt she had been associating with a woman who may, for all we know, be quite unsuitable for Tilly to know." Her eyes moistened with this new tribulation that had been heaped upon her. "So I want you to keep an eye on her for me."

Miles nodded. To obtain peace of mind he desperately needed to clear his conscience, tell tales on the sodden, dishevelled, near-mute child who had limped up on the hill. The words were gathering on his tongue, when his grandmother absently patted his head, and disappeared to join his grandfather.

*

Tilly, thwarted, misunderstood, falsely accused of misdemeanours of which she was not guilty, scowled, dredging up from her fertile imagination a variety of stratagems whereby she might escape to Fernwell Hospital, before inspiration burst: Mr. Pritchard! He'd tell her how Miss Madden was, maybe even give her a ride to the hospital on the back of his bike.

She chose her moment after lunch when her grandmother was settling the colonel for his afternoon rest and Miles was—helpful as always—clearing the dining-room table. This time, with practice, she slithered down the drain-pipe with more expertise, suffering no more damage to her person and clothes than a rip in the back of her shirt, and the skin scraped off one knuckle.

She walked forlornly down the short moss-coated path—even from a distance the cottage signalled its emptiness. When her knocking brought no response she ran to the back, hugging to herself the hope she'd see Mr. Pritchard. All that met her eye was scorched ragged grass stretching down to the boundary hedge, one half of which had been trimmed, the other abandoned by Mr. Pritchard for a cooler day. No sound reached her ears but the drone of a bee somewhere out of sight. She'd counted on finding him, kept her fingers crossed from the moment she'd jumped clear of the greenhouse. Cheated, she peered over the section of the hedge that had been cut in case Mr. Pritchard was behind it, rising up out of the ground to demand what she thought she was up to. But there was only a field in which three cows grazed.

She waited an hour and then disconsolately peered in each window, remembering the cake, the caramels and the sweet contentment she had shared with Miss Madden. For comfort she thought of Rufus, and the last three crosses that separated her from him. And Daddy! If she told him all about Miss Madden, he would understand, drive her to the hospital.

Hope reborn, Tilly was trudging back to Srinagar when, behind screens, a staff nurse in Fernwell Hospital was drawing the coarse sheet over Violet Madden's shrunken face. "Usual procedure, nurse. She registered her sister as next of kin, but it appears she's been dead for seven months! We're trying to contact her relatives, even a friend, but so far we've had no luck. I'll telephone the mortuary, ask them to hold her until we run someone to earth. Friendless, poor old soul. Makes you think, doesn't it?"

ELEVEN

Anna woke sprawled across the front seat of the car in an alien landscape, her throat dry and aching, her tongue too big for her mouth. No houses, no shops, only the blur of a green cul-de-sac that provided no clue as to her whereabouts. It was as though she'd been kidnapped and dumped while she slept. The dazzle of sunlight hurt her eyes, narrowed them to slits. Was it a sports ground, or a field? Was that dark shadow in the mid-distance a cricket pavilion or a cow shed?

Defeated, she sat behind the wheel, examined the stiff left hand, tried to flex it. The joints bent in a minuscule curve. She tested her left leg by willing it to thrust forward, but it remained as fixed as though it was planted in the floor of the car. Of their own accord her eyelids drooped and closed. Gradually, behind the dark screen a scene flickered into life: a bed, a cool, dimmed room where she could rest, sleep while her limbs recovered their mobility.

She steeled her will, switched on the ignition, the pressure of her good foot on the accelerator jerky and uncontrolled as she erratically manoeuvred the car round the green oblong onto a road. And there, on the horizon was a lode-star to guide her: the tall spire of Fernwell Parish church. Twice she missed her way, found herself on unfamiliar roads, but the beckoning promise of her own bed spurred her on.

She slithered through one set of traffic lights, stalled at another. Voices shouted abuse. From the curb a cyclist shook his fist at her. She refused to heed. Somewhere there was home, a haven from hooting cars, threatening fists. With a throb of relief, she recognised Anderbridge High Street. Now there was only a straight road between her and her bed.

Just ahead of Bateman's Lane was a cyclist. In a flicker of time he multiplied himself by two and then by three, a string of cycles reaching from one pavement to the other. She stamped on her brake, hit her forehead against the windscreen, as a cacophony of furious protest sounded at her rear. A motorist who'd by-passed her, stopped his car, lowered his window, and shouted at her.

Trapped in a hell on earth. Or was it a nightmare? Then, in some segment of her crippled brain she heard a whisper. Death! She was dying, in a street, where everyone reviled and threatened her, not caring whether she lived or died. As the cars circled her, with the last dregs of will-power she managed to swing the wheel, turn off the main road into Bateman's Lane. In the dappled peace, she laid her head on the steering wheel, unconscious of the tears that poured down her cheeks. After five minutes she drew herself upright: home was near now, no more than a few miles driving, and on the downward slope the car practically drove itself. It was then she saw the devil child, ambling along the verge, scuffling her feet, stuffing herself with blackberries, heedless of the approaching car. In a trice hate revitalised her, leaving her mind as clear as a bell. She could hear, see, and handle the car. She licked away the flecks of spittle that had oozed from the corners of her mouth, and with every atom of strength she possessed put her foot on the accelerator and in a screech of sound aimed the car, like a bullet, at the imp out of hell who, fists clenched to her chest stood transfixed with terror. She twisted round, started to run, but her feet couldn't fly fast enough to outdistance the car.

*

With the final piece that completed the jigsaw puzzle in his possession, Deacon gave a snort of satisfaction, drained the last inch of cold tea from the cup at his elbow. "That's it! Phone for the car, and we'll be on our way."

Warren held his tongue, made an effort to ignore the nag

that had been ticking in his head since Deacon—single-handed —had launched his blitzkrieg, failed. "Accepting a bribe doesn't constitute a crime, sir. We've no firm evidence of coercion. Only Masters' word. The old lady didn't name him."

Deacon, fussing over the exact placing of the reports in his folders, made no comment.

Warren ploughed on. "I agree it's pretty obvious that she made him a handsome present for the satisfaction of spitting in her son's eye. An uncle of mine was head gardener there, retired years ago, but he still remembers what an old curmudgeon Lady Masters was. Even when domestic help was available, she could never keep any staff."

Deacon wagged a thick admonishing finger in Warren's face. "£5,000 in cash, paid into his London bank, where—a bit of luck for us—he still kept a checking account even after he moved to Anderbridge. A week later he drew out £2,000, paid it into the Fernwell branch and, after waiting a fortnight handed a cheque for that amount into the Building Society, so cutting his mortgage commitment. The remainder he paid off in eighteen months, *and* modernised the property. Facts, boy, facts, down on paper, indisputable." He gave a derisory sniff. "You didn't know Garth Rampton very well, did you?"

"No, sir. Passed the time of day a few times, that's all."

"So you wouldn't know what his reaction would be to an employee who double-crossed him?" Warren opened his mouth to answer, but closed it as Deacon pontificated. "I'll tell you: He'd have fired him. Out, bag and baggage. And if any firm had asked him for a reference for Lang, he'd have refused point-blank to supply it. Once Arnold Masters had spilt the beans to him, Lang could have died in a gutter or rotted in prison for all Rampton cared."

He grinned sardonically. "What's bugging you and the few other clever dicks still hanging around is that we can't produce an eye-witness to murder! No fingerprints, not even a stray passer-by who saw him drive out of the parking yard. Only a senile old woman nattering about someone who'd run over her cat!"

"She died this morning, sir."

"So I was informed. Meanwhile, short of cast-iron evidence being handed to you on a plate, we'll have to put our wits to work, won't we?"

"Yes, sir."

"We leave in five minutes. Butts will bring the car round. Check the equipment I've ordered is aboard. Morris and Strawson will be in a second car five minutes behind us. They're to stop short of the house, find themselves some cover and await radio instructions from me."

*

Edmund saw the police car turn in the drive, pull up outside the garage, the two men in the rear seats near enough to identify. Without haste he drained his glass, set it down on the low rosewood table, made no effort to move until the bell rang. Then he rose, stretched to relax his taut muscles, brushed a particle of dust from his knee.

Imbued with a sense of theatre, he accepted without a tick of anxiety a confrontation from which, confident of his invulnerability, he knew he would emerge the winner. Hadn't he conceived and master-minded in minutes a murder which upward of twenty police officers hadn't the wits to solve? As he walked to the door he was rinsed clear of every vestige of fear.

In the second in which his finger hung over the latch, he reshaped his expression to one of courteous surprise at their unexpected arrival.

"Superintendent, Inspector Warren!" He hesitated a moment. "Do come in. I'll lead the way, shall I?" Without uttering a word, they followed at his heels. Edmund gestured towards the decanter and siphon. "May I pour you a drink?"

Deacon answered for both. "No thank you, sir."

Edmund invited them to sit down, which they did in upright chairs, and eyed them with mild curiosity. "Tell me how I can help you? I imagine you wouldn't be here if you weren't convinced I could be of some assistance to you."

"Exactly, sir." Deacon opted for a head-on approach. "We

have evidence that four years ago you received £5,000 from
the late Lady Masters. What favour warranted your accepting
that substantial sum of money?"

Edmund's brain raced. While not counting it a serious risk,
he had, as a final cautionary measure, prepared his defence. It
ran fluently off his tongue. "It was a private . . ." He corrected
himself. "I was about to say transaction, but that would be a
misnomer. It was a gift, a personal gift."

"You were on such terms with Lady Masters that out of
sheer generosity of heart she made you a present of £5,000?
That suggests your relationship with her was of long standing,
or that she was indebted to you for services you rendered."

"Not so, Superintendent. I only met her on three occasions.
She was an autocratic woman; her manner abrasive, hyper-
critical." He gazed in mild puzzlement at his two inquisitors.
"You may find what I am about to say difficult to believe, but I
swear it is the truth. She was a woman with few—if any—
friends, no knack of acquiring them. I can't explain why, but
an instant rapport established itself between us. She relished
gossip; like many elderly women living alone, she was inquisitive about other people's private lives. She was about mine, perhaps because at the time I met her she sensed it was at its
lowest ebb." For a second he experienced a spasm of fear that
his voice would fail him but he discovered if he used curt, short
sentences he could get by. "My wife had become infatuated
with another man . . . was pregnant by him. She asked me for
a divorce. The man concerned was my boss. So not only did I
lose my wife, but my job.

"On my second visit—Lady Masters had been considering
selling off some grazing land, but eventually decided against it
—she commented tartly that my shoes were down at heel, and
demanded to know why my wife didn't see that I was respect-
ably shod. I told her I no longer had a wife, the circumstances
of my divorce, its shattering effect on me. She asked me where
I was living. I told her. At that time this cottage was dilapi-
dated, not wholly weather-proof in winter, mortgaged to the

hilt. By some means she must have acquainted herself with its condition, my lack of funds.

"A week later she telephoned and summoned me to the Manor. After a drink she handed me a large envelope. A gift she said. Inside were £5,000 in treasury notes. Naturally somewhat stunned I refused to accept such a large sum of money. She said that her only child was as rich as Croesus, and as good as admitted that there was no love lost between them. We argued. I refused a dozen times, but to no effect. She was a supreme autocrat, deaf to any argument that was not in accord with her wishes. In the end, well, she wore me down, and I yielded to temptation. I'm not proud of the fact, but to the end of my life I'll be grateful for her generosity." He paused. "Who told you that Lady Masters made me a present of £5,000?"

"Her son. She had noted down the amount on a page in her diary, which, along with a considerable number of papers and documents, came into his possession after her death."

"And he resented it?"

"Naturally." Deacon shifted to spread his bulk more comfortably in the chair. "A gift, or a bribe?"

Edmund smiled. "I've explained. Surely I don't have to repeat myself?"

"I thought you might like to revise your statement. From some source—we won't pursue it at the moment—you learnt that Lady Masters proposed to sell the Manor House privately and was anxious to keep all knowledge of the transaction from her son. That is so, isn't it?"

"No, Superintendent. I had no knowledge whatsoever of her intentions."

He regarded Deacon without rancour or grudge, his inner self laughing at the first blazing rocket of luck that had ever come his way. Rose Nugent stranded at the side of the road, not a house or telephone within a mile, and two small children in the back of the car.

"In trouble?"

"Oh, yes. Bless you! I think it's the battery but I'm not sure. I'm a simpleton about the innards of cars."

He checked, but the car was an old banger with ten years' service behind it, beyond his skill to make roadworthy. "The quickest way to get you where you want to be is for me to drive you in my car to the nearest garage and ask them to collect yours. Take the keys out and hop in my car."

"Oh, you're an angel. If you wouldn't mind dropping the twins at their nursery school first, I'd be terribly grateful."

The luck fell into his lap when they were passing the pillared gates that led to the Manor House, just visible on the horizon, and the girl twin from the back seat boasted, "That's where we're going to live. Soon it'll be our house, and we'll have a swimming pool of our own and a great big one."

The sharp swing of Rose Nugent's head, the snap in her voice alerted him. "Hush, you remember what I told you."

"I know. It's a secret. But it won't always be a secret, will it, not when we're living there?"

"Your collar's rucked up. Straighten it. You're talking a lot of silly nonsense."

"But Granny Masters promised us that we'd live there. That we'd each have a pony . . ."

It was Rose Nugent's patent embarrassment, the panicky strictures to the girl child, the fact that she found it impossible to look him in the eye when they reached the garage that decided him. It was worth a try. Old Lady Masters gleefully plotting to spite a son it was common knowledge she detested.

The wizened monkey-face wore a grimace of contempt. "I pay you a sum of money or you will report to Rampton that I propose to sell the Manor House privately to a family of my choice. Am I correct?"

"Yes."

"You could go to gaol for blackmail."

"Always provided you've evidence of blackmail."

"How much?"

"Five thousand pounds."

"Get out."

He'd walked to the door, turned to face her. "Think it over."
And astonishingly she spat out, "I'll do just that."

Such was her depth of loathing for her son that, five days
later, she literally threw the envelope containing five thousand
pounds at Edmund's feet. "Damn you to hell! That's where
you'll end up."

Deacon interrupted the flashes of memory. "Not a bribe?"

"Certainly not. I was unaware that Lady Masters had
changed her mind, decided to sell the Manor House privately
to the Nugents until the news became public."

"Garth Rampton didn't attach any blame to you?"

"How could he? I had no inkling of her plans."

"Was he still in that frame of mind on the evening of the
night he was murdered, when he dropped in to see you at the
Anderbridge office?"

"By that time it was ancient history, Superintendent. Rampton wasn't the type to brood for four years on one sale that had
slipped through his fingers."

"Ancient history resurrected, Mr. Lang." The lie didn't cost
him a pang. "Dug alive out of a grave because while Arnold
Masters had been laid up he'd chanced to skim through his
mother's diaries, read a note of the amount of money you'd ex-
torted from her."

"I don't follow you, Superintendent. I have already explained that it was an outright gift. I agree, a remarkably generous one. But a gift none the less."

"Mr. Lang, I'm suggesting that on the night Rampton was
murdered, he drove to Anderbridge for one reason only: to fire
you. Throw you out, smash your cosy world. Without his back-
ing, you were unlikely to find another employer; certainly in
this county you'd have been black-listed." Deacon waved a
hand. "So good-bye to all this. It was him or you, Mr. Lang,
wasn't it? And you hadn't many options left open to you. In
fact, only two: silence Rampton, or have your career cave in
under you."

Edmund refused to be panicked by an ageing run-of-the-mill
policeman he despised. Deacon resorting to the time-worn trick

of threatening him with incriminating evidence he didn't possess. Harassment, then a slow wearing him down! They were out of luck. He shook his head, glanced in feigned bafflement from Deacon to Warren. "You're saying that I destroyed a human life, murdered in cold blood a man who was not only my employer, but my friend. It's a monstrous accusation, a . . ."

The telephone rang. Edmund crossed the room, lifted the receiver. "Edmund Lang."

There were dead moments of silence before he spoke. "Yes, I understand. I'll leave immediately for the hospital. I should be there in twenty minutes. Dr. Calvey, you say?"

He stood with his back to the two police officers, steadying his breath, striving for composure before he faced them. "Sorry, but I must cut this interview short. My sister has been involved in a car crash. She's in the hospital. I . . ."

"You have my sympathy," Deacon murmured. He snapped his fingers at Warren. "Have my car moved out of the driveway."

It wasn't until he'd almost reached the door that Edmund became aware that Deacon hadn't stirred in his chair. "If you wouldn't mind leaving."

"You get along. Don't hang about for us."

"I insist . . ."

"Don't think I should, sir, if I were you. You're hardly in a position to insist on anything. Also, first things first. You're urgently needed at the hospital."

Edmund suffered a resurgence of an old familiar pain: that flames were ripping through his body, and the fire would only be quenched when he'd slain his tormentor.

Deacon flapped his podgy hand. "Don't worry. We'll still be here when you get back with, I hope, good news of your sister."

Edmund's body went as rigid as though his bones were robbed of joints; a rictus of hate transformed his face into a mask. All that was left to him was his lungs. He could shout, scream. "Search the house, that's what you're determined to do, isn't it? And not for the first time! Go ahead. See where it gets you." He lurched out of the door, stumbled towards the garage. Anna. Anna. Whom he didn't love, but who was inextricably bound to him by the memories of their shared childhood, a mutual terror of a sadist who gloated over the miseries she had power to inflict upon them. Anna, a fixed star, an essential element in his life, a dead weight on his heart.

*

The middle-aged doctor rose behind his desk, held out his hand. "Please sit down, Mr. Lang."

"How is . . ." Edmund, his heart beating like a drum in his chest, was left with no breath to speak the final two words.

A thin man, with rumpled hair, spoke the professional words of sympathy. "Mr. Lang, I regret that I have to tell you that your sister is dead. There was really no hope when we admitted her, though we did our utmost."

Edmund stared at the knuckles in his lap, with a near irrepressible urge to bite them until the blood spurted from them as it had done in childhood. His nod of acknowledgment was barely visible.

The doctor walked to a cabinet on the far side of the room, poured brandy into a glass, wrapped Edmund's hand round it. "Not much solace, I know, but it will help. You've had a severe shock. Drink it."

Obediently, Edmund sipped. The doctor took a pen from the stand, held it suspended over a printed form.

"I appreciate this is very distressing for you, but I'm under an obligation to ask you a few questions. We have your sister's name and address on her driving licence, know she was a widow, but we need other data. I understand you are her next of kin."

Edmund nodded, managed to get four words off his tongue. "How did it happen?"

"We believe, though we can't be certain until after the autopsy, that she may have suffered a blackout or a stroke. The car was found on the right-hand side of Bateman's Lane, wedged into a bank. It may be that there was some mechanical fault in it, but we won't have the answer to that until it has been examined. No other vehicle was involved, but a child was severely injured. That means, of course, that the police are involved. There were some traces of alcohol in her blood, but not enough, in normal health, to warrant her losing control of the car. Now, if you wouldn't mind answering my questions."

Edmund did so. Anna was forty-two. She'd suffered the normal childish illnesses, had her appendix removed. Her doctor was Dr. Kenwood but as far as he knew she had not consulted him recently. Very occasionally she took a sleeping tablet, but never more than one.

"How often did you see your sister?"

"Frequently. Once, twice a week."

"She lived alone?"

"Yes."

"Had you noticed any deterioration in her health? For instance, was there even the slightest impediment in her speech? Were her movements sluggish? Did she suffer from minor blackouts?"

Edmund moistened his lips. "I don't understand."

"They could have been symptoms of ill-health of which she was not aware. Did you notice any?"

"No. None. Her health was excellent." Anna's sole guilt was that she had communed with the dead. A yearning to hold fast to the beloved. In an abyss of loneliness his heart wept. A child's face glimmered. Cradled in her hands was a beribboned birthday present on which she'd spent three months' pocket money.

He swallowed, blinked his eyes twice, and in some depth of his being found strength to meet the coolly enquiring eyes that seemed to require further assurance. "She behaved perfectly normally."

"Thank you. If you wouldn't mind signing the form."

Edmund handed it back to him. "May I see her?"

"Of course. One factor I would like to stress as it may be of some small comfort to you. She never recovered consciousness, suffered pain." He lifted the telephone, spoke softly into it, then rose, held out his hand. "Staff nurse Watkins will be here in a minute."

Beneath the head that was crowned with a helmet of bandages, the face was drained to a whitish-yellow as though all her blood had leaked out onto the roadside. He stood gazing down at her, seeing not the stranger's face, but a smaller one, transfixed with fear, who'd been viciously shaken until her teeth rattled, her cheeks slapped to a burning scarlet, and felt a warm liquid that could only be tears sliding down his cheeks.

"Thank you."

The nurse held open the door. "Would you like a cup of tea?"

He shook his head.

Leather-covered benches lined one of the walls. The nurse cupped his elbow. "Sit down for a minute or two. You're in shock, anyone would be. There! Now try taking a few deep breaths."

He opened and shut his mouth, but it had no effect.

"Are you sure you wouldn't like a cup of tea? It does help, you know."

He shook his head.

"Well, sit quietly, take it easy. We're short-staffed so I have to go back to my ward, but at the end of the corridor, to your left, there is a desk. Can you see it?"

He didn't even bother to look. "Yes."

"If you need a taxi to take you home, or anyone to be with you, the duty nurse will telephone for you." She patted his shoulder. "Okay?"

"Thank you."

The first of his senses to recover was that of smell: antiseptics, the nauseating stink of sweat on the woollen socks of the old man who occupied the other end of the bench. Then gradually, sight: the harsh fluorescent tube lighting, the nurses' uniforms, white-coated doctors, beds shuttling the deceased or dying to wherever they were being despatched.

He reared upright, a sickness heaving in his throat. "The way out?" he gulped to a nurse at the reception desk.

"Through the swing door, along the corridor, turn right and you'll see the lifts and the main staircase."

He chose the staircase because he could hold on to the banister-rail, regulate his pace. On the bottom step he looked through two glass doors into the parking yard. Beside his car, with his back to him, was a uniformed policeman. On guard over him, like a parcel to be returned to Deacon. With the reflex of a hunted animal, he wheeled, recalling by some quirk of memory, a door he'd seen open on to a fire-escape.

The third door he tried revealed an iron stairway running perpendicularly down into a yard choked with laundry vans. He was half a flight from ground level when a young constable emerged from behind a vehicle, gave him a thumbs up sign. His bones turned to water, were incapable of supporting him. His toe caught in the ironwork and he rolled over and over to sprawl half-stupefied on the tarmac.

The young policeman armed him up, brushed him down, all the while managing to keep a grip on his elbow. "All right, sir? Nasty tumble. Doesn't seem to be any bones broken. Better let us give you a lift home, sir. We'll collect your car later." And then, after a suitable pause, "Sorry to hear your sister's dead, sir."

For a moment in which his sight was impaired by iridescent flashes, he saw his hands gripped in a stranglehold on the constable's throat. But as he lifted one hand, his grazed knuckles dripping blood, a second constable stepped briskly to his side. With smiles, even some concern, they man-handled him into the police car.

*

Deacon walked round and round his prize exhibit, reluctant to take his eyes off it. "Not so downhearted now, are we! Got our evidence, haven't we?"

"It would seem so, sir."

"Seem so," Deacon roared. "It is so." He eyed Warren sourly. "Show a bit of enthusiasm, lad. It's a fine cop. Think themselves clever, these so-called brainy types, but they always make

one mistake. And he made his. In too much of a hurry. Made a
botched job of it."

"Yes, sir." Warren, a puritan at heart, hated a boaster. Satisfaction in justice was one thing, open glee another.

Deacon slightly re-arranged his exhibit, altered the angle of
the chair so that it faced the open door. "Wonder what lies
he'll dream up. Not that they'll land him anywhere but in gaol.
Ah, that's him." Deacon wiped the smile off his face, assumed
an appropriate expression of gravity.

Edmund walked ahead of the two sets of footsteps, brushing
the dust off his suit, re-aligning his cuffs. He'd already wiped
his knuckles clean of blood. Now all he had to do was to
unclench his teeth, moisten his lips. He had been absent from
the house for a little over an hour, during which they'd poked
and pried, for all he knew ransacked his home. Into his heart
that was as cold and dark as an icy night seeped tear-drops of
warmth, as he listened to the apology that Deacon would have
to force through his lips.

On the threshold of the room he was confronted by the plastic mac draped ceremoniously over a chair, dripping filthy
water on to his dove-grey carpet. For a split second the sacrilege
of the spoiled carpet took precedence over the significance of
the mac. "How dare you?" he raged, a curtain of scarlet rising
behind his eyes. "Wreck my home, spread filth?"

Deacon pointed to the draped chair. "Yours, sir, I believe.
Not sufficient weight for your purpose, I'm afraid. In time it
becomes inflatable. Air pockets form in the sleeves and then it
rises to the surface."

"What are you suggesting? It's not mine."

"I think it is, sir. Protective clothing. Pair of rubber gloves
too. Mint condition. You don't know much about wells, do
you, sir. Fickle things. Can't depend on them, not in this part
of the country, nor what effect a prolonged drought has on
them. I'll tell you what it does, drains them. Your well, like another along the road, hasn't more than five feet of water in it.
It's fed from a spring up in the hills and a stream. But for a
month the spring's been as dry as a bone, and the stream is re-

duced to a trickle. So tomorrow we propose to go fishing. There'll be a lot of old rubbish, but what we'll be looking for is a gun. And we'll find it."

Edmund let out a single scream, sprang at Deacon, knuckles clenched to beat him to pulp. Deacon who, for a heavy man, was light on his feet, dodged as Warren seized Edmund's wrists, twisted them behind his back.

"Meanwhile," Deacon went on, ignoring the threat to his person, "we'll return to the station where you'll be formally cautioned and you can, if you so choose, make a statement. You are also entitled to one telephone call if you wish to consult a solicitor."

*

Tilly, sitting in a wheel-chair, waited impatiently for her father's comment on the letter she already knew by heart.

He returned it to her outstretched hand, dropped a kiss on her domed forehead. "My, what a testimonial! I think we should frame it, don't you?"

"Detective Inspector Warren brought it soon after you'd gone this afternoon. And a super box of chocolates." She pointed to one of the dozen signatures scrawled on the white plaster. "And he signed my cast. Look! Anthony Cyril Warren."

He looked. "What the police call a commendation. They don't often hand them out, but you earned it."

"Yes, I did, didn't I, because I found the dead man."

"Yes."

The glow of mingled triumph and pride slid off her face. "But I never saw the weasel again."

"It's probably moved house." He tapped the tip of her nose. "If you remember trespassers are prosecuted in that wood, so it's out of bounds for us forever more. We'll have to find another site for our weasel-hunting." He glanced at his watch. "Honey, I have to go. That grey-haired nurse has already signalled to me three times it's long past visiting hours. I only slipped in for a minute to say good night."

Not heeding, Tilly said, "I'm glad the witch is dead, but I

wish you'd seen her. She had fangs and blood dripped off her fingers."

His eyes traced the line of stitches on the left side of her skull where a band of white skin had been shaven of its silky raven hair, the leg encased in plaster. "Maybe it's just as well I didn't!"

"She'll be in hell now, won't she, with devils prodding her with red-hot toasting forks?" The unholy glee faded, and her voice trembled. "But Miss Madden will be in heaven, won't she?"

Gazing down into the small beseeching face he was at a loss to understand how a child brought up in an agnostic home, attending a school that allocated thirty minutes per week to religious instruction, had acquired an implicit faith in the hereafter. "Yes, darling. At peace, no more worries, no more getting hurt. That's how people are when they are dead."

She gripped his hand. "But she's not there yet. I asked one of the nurses, the nice one with red hair. They're not going to put Miss Madden into her grave until tomorrow."

"And we're all going home tomorrow. Remember? That's why Mummy telephoned Mrs. Hunt and asked her to ferry Rufus over, so he'll be there almost as soon as we are."

"I know." Without warning, tears brimmed over her eyelids. "Daddy, she had a little cat, a tabby, with green eyes, but it was run over and killed. Supposing it had been Rufus!" The tears gathered momentum, tumbling down her cheeks.

Gently he wiped them away. "It's sad, darling, I know."

She sniffed, blew her nose. "They have flowers at funerals, don't they? When Mr. Harrison next door died, Mummy said you couldn't see the coffin for wreaths. Daddy, please, I want Miss Madden to have some flowers. Could you buy her a great big, beautiful wreath? She'd love it, I know she would."

"If you want me to."

"Oh, I do. Please, Daddy."

"Okay. The shops will be shut by now, but I'll order it on my way here in the morning."

23

"With lots of pink ribbon and a card. Pink was her favourite colour."

"With pink ribbon and a card. What do you want me to write on the card?"

She pondered for a whole minute, then announced solemnly, "To my best friend with love from Tilly."

He repeated the words after her, kissed the tip of her nose. "Sleep tight, honey. Mummy, Miles and I will be here to collect you at half past nine. So mind you're ready. With luck we'll be home by lunchtime."

She shot him a look of alarm. "But not straight home. I must go to Granny's first."

"But you said good-bye to her this afternoon."

"I don't want to see *her*. Just to go into the greenhouse to dig up your present."

He looked baffled. "A present! It's not my birthday. And anyway why did you bury it?"

"To keep it safe from the witch, where she'd never find it, ever. The most beautiful present you've ever had."

"But what is it?"

"It's a surprise." She clapped her hands. "Promise we can dig it up before we go home. Promise!"

The severe-faced nurse tapped his shoulder. "Mr. Allenby, it's past visiting hours, high time Tilly was in bed."

"Yes, I know. I do apologise. I'm just leaving."

As he stood up, Tilly grabbed his hand. "You're not to tell anyone it's in the greenhouse, and you're to promise, on your honour, we can go and dig it up in the morning before we go home. Cross your heart?"

"Cross my heart."

Waving to him, her heart overflowing with the joy of giving, she hugged like a treasure the thought of the moment to come when she would blow the cobwebs off the gold watch and lay it in the palm of her father's hand.